SPA
DEADLY

Things are rough at the resort. In fact, they're murder.

SPA DEADLY

An Allie Armington Mystery

LOUISE GAYLORD

NATIONAL AWARD-WINNING AUTHOR

Little Moose Press
Beverly Hills, California

Little Moose Press
269 S. Beverly Drive, Suite #1065
Beverly Hills, CA 90212
866-234-0626
www.littlemoosepress.com

Library of Congress Cataloging-in-Publication Data

Gaylord, Louise.

     Spa deadly : an Allie Armington mystery / Louise Gaylord. — 1st ed.
     p. cm.
     ISBN 978-0-9720227-1-2 (hardcover : alk. paper)
     1. Armington, Allie (Fictitious character)—Fiction. 2. Women lawyers—Fiction. 3. Health resorts—Fiction. 4. New Mexico—Fiction. I. Title.

PS3607.A986S63 2008
  813'.6—dc22   2008015431

Dust jacket and book design: Dotti Albertine
Interior layout: Ghislain Viau
Map: Lewis Agrell
Author photo: Christian Cooper

Printed in the United States of America on acid-free paper.

Little Moose Press is committed to protecting the environment and to the responsible use of natural resources. As a book publisher, with paper a core part of our business, we are concerned about the future of the world's remaining endangered forests and the environmental impacts of paper production. We are committed to implementing policies that will support the preservation of endangered forests globally and advance best practices within the book and paper industries.

Books are available at quantity discounts when used to promote products or services. For information please email Little Moose Press.

To Missy

CHAPTER 1

MY SISTER, ANGELA, AND I have been impatiently waiting in the baggage area of the Albuquerque airport for the late American flight out of Dallas to arrive.

Finally, we see the Cielo Azul Spa driver, lugging a bulky leather briefcase, followed by a tall, thin woman, her ash blonde hair pulled back in a chic chignon and a determined scowl etched into her face.

I do a double take. There's something about her that sends a shivering shudder down my spine. It's her eyes. I know those eyes. I can't remember where I've seen them, but, deep down in my gut, I know this woman means trouble.

Several steps behind her lurches a short, pretty, but slightly overweight woman with enormous brown eyes. Her spiky, auburn-streaked hair reminds me of a tossed radicchio salad.

When the first woman reaches us, I stand and extend my hand. "Hi. I'm Allie Armington from Houston, and this is my sister, Angela Bruce."

The woman ignores me and edges past to speak in lowered tones to the driver, now loading a cart with several pieces of luggage. Once he's done, he looks our way, frowns, then waves us to follow.

The little round lady grabs my hand and gives it an extended shake, as her words gush. "Hey there, I'm Rebbie Dalton from Tulsa, Oklahoma. The Rebbie's short for Rebecca. Boy, am I glad to see you two."

She pitches a furtive nod in the skinny blonde woman's direction and whispers, "I had to sit next to that bitch in first class all the way from Dallas. What a pain in the patooty. All she talked about was how she's going to close the biggest deal of her life. I tried self-medicating with four Bloody Marys, but they didn't help one bit."

I give an involuntary shiver as I nod my agreement. "She looks like she could be quite a handful."

"You got that right. How long are you staying?"

"A week, but even that seems like a life sentence."

She lets out a long sigh. "I've signed up for two. Hope I didn't make a mistake."

Once we reach a forest green Lincoln Navigator with "Cielo Azul Spa" painted on the side, the driver steps toward me.

"Pardon, ma'am, but—," he jerks a thumb toward the woman and mutters, "the lady requested that you and your sister take the rear seat. Seems she suffers from motion sickness."

Not a wise move. After nine long months, seventeen hours of unproductive labor, and a C–section, honeymoon baby Duncan Bruce the Third, fondly referred to as "D3," finally arrived.

As a result, Angela's hormones are still majorly out of whack and when my sister's chin juts as her mouth hardens into a thin, red line, I know she's squaring off for a fight.

Before she can get the first word out of her mouth, I shove her toward the back of the SUV. "Not a hill to die on."

Rebbie Dalton is forced to share the second row with the woman because the front passenger seat has been tilted forward to accommodate that enormous leather briefcase.

The minute we pull away from the curb, the woman punches a number on her cell, waits a few seconds, then screams that she doesn't give a good goddamn if it's nearly 2:00 a.m. in New York;

she needs the information now. Too damn bad if he has to go to the office—she expects a lot of faxes when she arrives at the spa. "And they better be there, or it's your ass."

Her diatribe continues as we speed up I-25 to take 599 past Santa Fe, and then turn northeast toward Taos at Española.

Either the cell runs out of juice or the woman runs out of steam, because blessed silence finally fills the car. Not that it matters. Angela has been snoring into my shoulder for more than an hour, and Rebbie Dalton's bobbing head has totally disappeared.

I let out a long sigh and stare out the window into the headlights of the oncoming cars. A vision of the woman sitting in front of me nags at the side of my brain. Where have I seen her? Why can't I remember?

This trip has been a bad idea from the very get-go. How could I have let my sister muscle me into acceptance, especially after the unannounced arrival of Bill Cotton, my fiancé?

Bill and I were almost strangers again since we had communicated only by phone after our week together following Angela's wedding on the North Shore.

Promised winter and spring weekends were set aside for good reasons, and then he had gone incommunicado for most of the summer, busting a major drug cartel based in the Lesser Antilles.

After spending several days devoted to the joys of rediscovery, Bill announced he needed his own space and rented a nearby studio apartment on a street between San Felipe and Westheimer.

Before I had time to lodge a protest, the baby arrived and my auntly attentions turned to him.

Problem was, Bill didn't seem to mind at all that he was put on the back burner. And, now that I think about it, he actually seemed relieved that he wasn't included in the family festivities.

Not that I blame him. My parents were not overly welcoming, and Angela and Duncan hardly acknowledged him.

Still, when it came time to depart, Bill treated me to a delicious dinner for two at Tony's, during which he plied me with wine. After spending the evening in my bed, wrapping me in the comfort of his arms, he planted a lingering farewell kiss and then whispered, "Your sister needs you. Suck it up. It's only a week."

The outskirts of Taos are less than inviting—one strip mall after another—but the heart of the town is mostly classic Pueblo architecture featuring softly rounded adobe buildings with heavy timbers, known as *vigas*, extending through the outside walls as main roof support beams.

A few minutes later, we pass signs pointing to the Taos Pueblo and the Rio Grande Gorge Bridge, then turn right on the Taos Ski Valley Road. Just past Arroyo Seco, we head east on a poorly paved Taos County road and begin to climb.

As the Navigator careens dizzily up one narrow switchback after another, I check my seat belt and stare into the inky night.

It's then I curse my sister for making such a dumb decision about her unborn child. It was in August when Angela, worn out from the pregnancy, had been so positive she would need this time to recuperate. But that was then—before D3 came into our lives and stole our hearts away.

CHAPTER 2

WHEN THE NAVIGATOR ROLLS to a stop, I open one eye. A man in uniform is leaning in the window with a clipboard, checking off names as the driver recites the list. Behind him is a kiosk, its interior banked with television monitors.

After the guard checks his list, he says, "Welcome to Cielo Azul, ladies. Have a nice stay."

I'm wide awake by the time the Navigator pulls in front of the main lodge. Wide awake enough to notice the blond guy who meets the car and points the tall, thin woman toward the main office.

I check the man out for a second time. He's over six foot, with bulging biceps, great pecs, and a tight butt. And I can tell that he knows it because he's acting like he's the last Coca-Cola in the desert.

After he gathers our luggage and places it on an elongated golf cart, he drives the Dalton woman, Angela, and me the short distance to our separate cabins.

We wait on the cart as Rebbie is ushered into Cabin Two. After almost fifteen minutes, he emerges with a wide but apologetic smile smeared across his face.

"Pardon for the delay. Miz Dalton had trouble unlocking her suitcase."

When Angela enters Cabin Three, she protests, saying she requested a double. The hunk shrugs. "Sorry, ma'am, unless you're with a man they book you into a single cabin. Talk to someone at the spa desk tomorrow. Maybe they'll make an exception and you can change."

He shows me to Cabin Four, places my suitcase on the luggage stand, and then motions to a plate of fruit and a bottle of water on a small table.

"Breakfast is served in the main dining room from six to nine. Weather permitting, lunch is on the dining terrace from one to two thirty. Dinner's in the main dining room beginning at seven.

"No wine, liquor, or cell phones are allowed in the public areas, but there is a wine list available for in-room dining, and you can make all the cell calls you want from your cabin.

"Please go over your schedule before you retire. You'll be receiving one each evening for the following day."

He backs toward the door and points to the name stitched on his shirt pocket. "If I can do anything for a fellow Texan, don't hesitate to ask for Tex. Tex Bodine."

I hold up my hand. "Actually, there is something I'm a little curious about. Do you happen to know the name of the very tall woman who arrived with us tonight? She looks very familiar—especially around the eyes."

He pulls a card from his pocket. "Listed here as Selena Channing. Says she's a first-timer just like the three of you. She's booked into Cabin Nine. But I don't think she'll be getting much sleep. There were over thirty fax pages waiting at the front desk."

After Tex shuts the door, it doesn't take long to unpack my suitcase and check out my suede backpack purse.

I pull out my cell. Though there's plenty of signal, Angela—who depleted the battery on her cell by the time we got to Albuquerque—has managed to use up my entire battery as well.

After I plug in the charger, I check the purse for my holstered Beretta Tomcat 3032, a gift from my dad when I joined the Harris County DA's office several years before. Then I pitch the purse onto the topmost shelf of the closet.

Transporting a weapon by air is a nuisance, but, since I'm licensed to carry a concealed firearm and used to having it with me, I never leave home without my trusty little friend.

The few extra minutes to show my passport, the license, and check the Beretta to my final destination have been well worth my peace of mind.

To quote one of Quentin Tarantino's movie characters, "Better to have a gun and not need it than it is to need a gun and not have it."

I reach for the telephone. Okay, so it's past two. Bill can sleep in tomorrow morning.

It's then I see the folded card on the bedside table noting that, in respect for client privacy, all calls to the rooms, incoming and outgoing, are routed through the switchboard, which opens at seven and closes at ten. At the bottom, in block letters, is a reminder that cells are permitted only in the cabins.

Disappointed, I settle beneath the coverlet and pick up the card printed with my schedule:

Monday

6-9	a.m.	Breakfast in the Main Dining Room
8	a.m.	Nigella Devering, Spa Director
8:30	a.m.	Meet Your Physical Trainer
9	a.m.	Massage: Marva
10	a.m.	Medical Conference: Dr. Tole
11	a.m.	Broth by the Pool
1	p.m.	Lunch

Today your afternoon is free to hike, rock climb, or try a comfortable lounge beside our Sacred Pool. Schedules change daily, so be sure to check yours each evening.

Nigella Devering? There can be only one Nigella Devering. And there's going to be trouble when Angela finds out. This could ruin the entire week.

CHAPTER 3

DAYLIGHT STREAMING through the window above my bed pulls me out of an exhausted sleep.

My first act is to grab my newly charged cell and get in touch with Bill on his. He's positive landlines will soon go the way of the buggy whip, so the only means of communicating with him is through his cell.

The sound of his sleep-laden voice surrounds me like velvet. "Hey there, love. I take it you made it?"

I can't help but laugh. "Yes, we made it, but it was past midnight. The plane from Dallas was late. Lucky for you, Angela used up all the juice in my cell talking to Duncan, or I would have called you then. I miss you already."

"Same here. But am I glad you called when you did. You saved my ass. Can't talk now. I have an appointment downtown. I'll call when I get back."

I shove aside my disappointment at Bill's quick brush-off to take a shower, then pull on a spa-issue forest green sweat suit and head out for a brief tour.

Cielo Azul is a marriage of rustic log exteriors with Pueblo-style interiors. Though it sounds odd, the combination actually works.

The main lodge, a two-story living and dining area, features the same décor my cabin boasts—whitewashed plaster walls, tastefully adorned with R.C. Gorman paintings interspersed with other Navajo works, Saltillo tile floors, and ceilings composed of *vigas* separated by crosspieces of small strips of wood known as *latillas*.

Fireplaces so large one can almost stand inside them fill the two narrower walls, and a huge picture window frames an ever-green forest dotted with clusters of exuberant yellow aspens and dominated by a tall peak.

I smell coffee, and sniff my way to a discreetly placed alcove off the living area. A large flat-screen wall-hung TV hovers above a long table with carafes of coffee labeled with exotic names: Jamaica Blue, Guiana French Roast, Costa Rican Mild.

I pour a cup and take a sip while I read the CNN crawl at the bottom of the screen.

Angela's going to be furious to learn there is a TV available in the main lodge, but with no apparent access to her soaps. When she discovered there was no television in the cabins, she almost went over the edge.

She'll be missing a whole week of *As the World Turns* and is too embarrassed to phone home and ask someone to TiVo it.

A small brass plaque to the right of double glass doors directs me to the spa and workout rooms hidden in the woods behind the main lodge. Otherwise, the only indication there might be outer buildings is a wide trail lined with aspens that leads into the woods.

Once there, I make my way into an attractive meeting room dotted with conversation clusters featuring overstuffed chairs and sofas that look so comfortable, I'm tempted to sink into the buttery leather and spend the rest of the day.

Even at this early hour, the spa reception desk is a hive of activity. Five uniformed personnel, including the blond hunk who showed us to our rooms earlier this morning, attend to a line of guests, clad in fluffy dark green bathrobes, paused to register before entering the doors to the women's or men's facilities.

I breakfast at the community table with two very glamorous Hollywood-type couples wearing designer sunglasses. They must be important because they barely acknowledge my presence.

It's a little before eight o'clock when I return to the spa for my appointment with Nigella.

I've already flipped through several magazines when I notice the wall filled with photographs of the Cielo Azul staff. Beneath the picture of a pale but attractive white-blonde, the nameplate reads: "Nigella Devering, Spa Director."

The years have been kind to her. Though she's more mature than I remember, of course, her smile is exactly the same. There is, however, a definite wistfulness in those eyes.

Nigella, who joined Angela's class in the ninth grade, was a cotton-topped, pasty-faced girl with an English accent.

The kids teased her about her peculiar speech and grabbed at the Coke-bottle glasses that were forever sliding down her nose. But, worse than that, though most of us wore braces, Nigella was clueless about brushing after meals. When anybody mentioned "Food Face," we all knew who they meant.

I check my watch yet again. 8:25. Nigella must have forgotten our appointment. Michelle, my physical trainer, is next on my list at eight thirty.

Since I'm a real stickler for being on time, I head to the spa director's door and raise my hand to knock.

That's when I hear Nigella say, "But I don't understand. My father meant this to be our legacy."

When another woman replies, "That might have been true at one time, when your father was managing partner," I immediately recognize who it is. Selena Channing is on the other side of that door.

"Unfortunately for us at the bank, as well as for you, your father's death greatly changed our interests in SpaCo. So, if we can't come to some sort of agreement—and soon—you and your brother stand to lose not only a potful of money, but both spas as well."

I take a quick step back from the door, embarrassed that I have inadvertently eavesdropped. Then I hurry out of the office, through the door marked "Women's Spa," and down the long, dark hall past the treatment rooms, to the gym.

CHAPTER 4

THE VAST ROOM filled with weight machines and treadmills is empty except for a trainer and an attractive man with a heavy mane of silver-streaked brown, pushing a stationary bike to the limit. There's not a bead of sweat on his narrow, aristocratic face, and his measured breathing tells me he is used to this kind of physical exertion.

When he looks up and smiles, I have a vague feeling that I should know him. A very uneasy feeling.

He reaches for the forest green towel held by the statuesque brunette standing next to him, then dismounts to tower above her. "Thank you, my friend."

At the sound of his voice, an icy sliver of recognition slides through me. Here is the one man I never expected to see again: Ramón Talavera, head of one of the most powerful crime families in Mexico.

The last news I had of Talavera was that he was to be extradited and stand trial in El Paso.

I'm sure he's not happy to see me. Thanks to my testimony, his cousin Raymond Gibbs is serving a stiff sentence for his part in Talavera's drug operation.

Yet here he stands with a smile and extended hand. And, because I have little choice but to place mine in his, I watch as, in his customary fashion, he turns my hand to brush it lightly with his lips.

"Miss Armington, what an enjoyable surprise. How are you?"

I recover my wits enough to go along with the ancient ritual. "I'm just fine, Señor Talavera, and you?"

"How kind of you to ask. We are all fine except for my dear cousin Ray who, unfortunately, is languishing in a not-so-very-nice place near Milan"—he pauses, then adds—"New Mexico."

I decide that it would be in my best interest to skirt Ray Gibbs's imprisonment. "And how is your lovely wife?"

He flashes a toothy grin. "My Nita is the reason we are here. She recently presented me with our fifth child, Raoul. He is our third son."

I have to bite my tongue to keep from saying, "Goody, goody, yet another generation of *narcotraficantes* waiting in the wings."

Ramón steps away and turns to the brunette. "Adios, my beauty. We will be leaving shortly. Thank you for your interest in my welfare and"—he pauses just long enough to make it clear that he and the woman most probably have been intimate—"your support."

He nods my way, then strides out the door of the gym.

The brunette waits until Talavera exits, then turns to me. "Right on time, Miss Armington. Sorry for the small delay. Señor Talavera and his wife are longtime clients of the spa. I wish all our clients could be as wonderful as those two are."

The woman sticks out her hand. "I'm Michelle."

"Do you know who that man is?"

Michelle smiles. "Of course, he is Señor Talavera."

Then I add, "Of the Talavera cartel."

She laughs and shakes her head. "Oh, goodness, no. They're not even related. From what I gather *this* Señor Talavera has lots of different businesses. I know he owns a winery in Parras, Coahuilla, because he brought me a lovely bottle of Talavera brandy last July. And then there are the gas wells. Or maybe it's oil. But, whatever he does, he must make a lot of money because he has several jets."

I bite my tongue. No point in trying to get the truth out. She's bought in, hook, line, and sinker.

Michelle motions me through open doors into the aspen-filled courtyard where a gentle breeze moves through dancing golden leaves. After taking a deep breath, she gives me a warm and welcoming smile. "I just love the fall colors, don't you? Here. Have a seat."

Once I'm down, she gracefully settles on a bench, pulls out a sheet from her file, and locates a ballpoint. "Age?"

I peer over the top of the sheet and read the questions upside down. "Thirty-three. Single. Five foot ten, one hundred thirty-five pounds. Moderately active. Play scratch golf when I have the time. And I'm a practicing attorney."

"Wow. That was fast." Michelle places the sheet back in her folder. "You seem to be in pretty good shape. What do you want to work on?"

I want to say, "To look like you," but that's pointless. As pointless as wanting to look like my older sister, Angela—the beautiful one.

Even though I have nice gray eyes, an engaging smile, and even, white teeth, my genes miss drop-dead gorgeous. No, I'm not ugly by a long shot, but, next to my sister, I've always felt plain.

Instead, I say, "Thanks for the compliment. To be honest, I wouldn't be here if it weren't for my sister. She delivered her first baby several weeks ago. I was the lucky one nominated to keep her company."

"Too bad your sister won't get to meet Nita Talavera. She looks great in spite of having five babies in almost as many years."

Not as far as I'm concerned. The sooner the Talaveras adios this place, the better I'll feel.

Michelle points to the gym. "Instead of using the treadmills and the other aerobic equipment, you might be interested in the climbing wall. It's our newest feature. They tore out the end of the gym last month and put in a thirty-foot scale. Absolutely fabulous."

"I've never climbed. Looks hard."

"It is—at first. Of course, we have state-of-the-art belaying ropes and harnesses, and all clients are spotted by a staff person from the minute they leave the floor.

"Just be sure to book a climb time at least twenty-four hours in advance. Only four clients are allowed on the wall per session, which lasts between twenty-five to thirty minutes."

"That doesn't seem very long."

She smiles. "It is when you're a beginner. The gym opens at 5:00 a.m. and is fully staffed from then until it closes at nine."

I size up the situation and decide thirty minutes on a fake wall comes in a distant third to enjoying the beauties of nature. "Maybe later. I'm more interested in the trails."

"You're not the only one. We have several clients who fly in just for the hikes. In fact, Cielo Azul has so many different trails, it's impossible to cover them all in a single visit."

"I have a week."

"That would be a stretch."

She slips a map from a pocket in her folder, spreads it on the bench, and motions me in.

"There's a copy of this map in your room, but sometimes they get legs." She uncaps a pen. "Forget the trails marked in green. Except for—"

She marks a wide green line. "Even though Lágrima Del Sol is designated Beginner, it quickly turns into Intermediate, and leads to most of the more difficult blue diamond trails.

"I'd do the right side of the map first. The views are spectacular. Save the trails on the left side of the map for another time."

Then Michelle raises a warning hand. "The only thing Cielo Azul requests is that, when you do go for a hike, you let Spa Reception know the trails you'll be taking."

I fold the map and pocket it, then say, "How often do the Talaveras come to Cielo Azul?"

Michelle studies the ground for a second, then looks me square in the eye. "I don't want to seem rude, but we aren't allowed to give out specific information about our clients. That means I've probably said too much already."

CHAPTER 5

FROM NINE TO TEN, I spend my first delicious hour beneath the hands of my masseuse.

Much to my dismay, however, though Marva is a grandmotherly sort with a pleasant round face, she's also a seamless talker. As she pommels and smoothes, she babbles on about her worthless sloth of a son who showed such promise in high school but took the wrong path after college when he went to work for the casino down in Española.

I try to block her drivel by conjuring up Bill, imagining his lips on mine, his body against mine, his hands searching.

But Marva's words keep tumbling from above. "After all I did for him after his father walked. Worked two jobs. Sacrificed my social life. And how does he pay me back?"

Things perk up when Marva turns her attentions to the latest staff gossip. She saves the juiciest tidbit for last. "We've already lost one couple because of that loudmouth, Miz Channin'. They said she destroyed the karma of the place. You know those Californians and their karma."

She mangles my right arm and then smoothes it out.

"They wanted their money back but had to leave empty-handed."

Marva moves to my left side, whips the sheet back over my arm, then exposes my left leg. She picks up my foot and sends me to heaven. There is nothing like reflexology.

After she works on several pressure points, she manages to get out, "The only one at the spa with the combination to the safe is Miz Deverin', and she's not here."

I perk up at that one when I realize, not an hour ago, I heard her voice on the other side of her office door. "Miss Devering is away?"

"Happens every week or so. The company jet picks her up Monday, and she comes back Tuesday. Sometimes she flies clients in. Sometimes she takes clients to the island. Rumor is this spa's in some financial trouble, but the sister-spa off Baja is really suckin' air."

Since Marva is seemingly very willing to trade information, I decide a little probing won't hurt.

"Do you know the Talaveras? I just met him a few minutes ago in the gym."

Her hands smooth up and down my back. "Sure, I know them. They're some of the spa's most frequent clients. The mister comes at least once a month. Big buddies with Miz Deverin'."

CHAPTER 6

THE TEN O'CLOCK MEDICAL CONFERENCE with Dr. Tole and his nurse/wife is brief. He's attractive, with a crew cut, and resembles a thinner version of the Marlboro Man.

Beneath the standard starched white coat, Tole wears a plaid shirt, jeans with a big silver and turquoise belt buckle, and working cowboy boots. All he needs is a Stetson.

He writes down my info while his wife, an attractive redhead with a dazzler smile, takes my temperature and blood pressure.

"Single?" He flashes me a wide grin and drawls, "You're much too purty to be a single gal."

When his wife stops pumping the blood-pressure cuff, his smile flattens. "What's the reading?"

"One ten over sixty-five."

Tole pats me on the back. "Guess that's all. Enjoy your stay."

I turn to go, then stop. "Mind if I ask you a question or two?"

His face brightens. "Sure."

"Do you live around here?"

"No. We're in Taos, but we come up on Mondays to check out the new clients, then we're on call for Walking Rain the rest of the week."

"Walking Rain?"

The wife jumps in, but it sounds like she's reading copy. "Walking Rain is for groups only. Those particularly interested in the metaphysical approach. That's why we signed on. Mike and I are devotees."

"So you have a practice in Taos?"

Tole smiles. "Sure do. But I've been limiting my patients in order to take this job. We plan to move someplace out here at the beginning of next year. That way I'll have more time for the fall hunting season."

"What's your specialty?"

"Deer and turkey. I favor the bow, but a rifle will do just as well."

The wife doesn't seem quite as enthusiastic. "We'll see about that move."

The tension between the two fills the room. Somebody's not happy. And I can guess who.

Finally I say, "I arrived late last night, so other than going through Taos, I have no idea where I am."

Tole says, "This is Carson National Forest, and the mountains are the Sangre de Cristo."

"Blood of Christ? That's an odd name."

"Not if you see them at sunset. Deep red. The mountain you see from the dining room is Wheeler Peak, the tallest in New Mexico. And the mountain to the right of Wheeler is Taos Mountain. No one is allowed on that land but Taos Pueblo members. That mountain is sacred to their tribe."

I'm at the door when I remember Talavera. "I met a very nice man in the gym this morning, a Mr. Talavera? Do you happen to know him?"

The two lock eyes for only a second, but I catch it before the wife wheels away to stow the blood-pressure cuff.

Tole puts on a puzzled look and shakes his head. "Talavera? No. Can't say we do. But then we've only been here since the spa opened for the season at the beginning of the month."

CHAPTER 7

I CHECK MY WATCH. I have over an hour before I'm to meet Angela for lunch, so I hotfoot it back to my cabin to find the brochure touting the amenities of Cielo Azul:

> Located in the Carson National Forest north of the charming hamlet of Arroyo Seco, **Cielo Azul** hosts sixty clients pampered by twice as many attendants.

> The newest addition to **Cielo Azul** this season is Walking Rain Retreat House, located in a secluded spot of enormous beauty and tranquillity.

> Walking Rain offers groups complete privacy and anonymity. Features include in-house dining, special menus, and medical supervision.

I skim over the rest of the hype, then turn to the back and read the blurb on the sister spa.

Ola Azul:
Located just off lower Baja near Punta Ventana is our newly acquired sister-spa. This island paradise features five sand beaches and a blue lagoon

surrounded by swaying palms. Twenty secluded cabañas promise ultimate privacy only a minute's walk from our cutting-edge spa. Our best-kept secret: a landing strip long enough to accommodate mid-sized private jets.

At the bottom, the brochure says,

Cielo Azul & Ola Azul: properties of SpaCo, Ltd.
Closed: September

No prices are listed for either facility. I guess if you have to ask, you can't afford it.

I grab my cell, get on the net, and Google "SpaCo." Not much info, except it is a privately held offshore corporation with a post office box in Georgetown, Grand Cayman.

I punch in Bill's cell number. When his message comes on, I wait for the beep. "Hey. It's me. Where have you been? I've been trying to get you since this morning.

"First. You are not going to believe who I ran into this morning. Ramón Talavera. Whatever happened with him? The last thing I heard, he was to be extradited and tried in El Paso. I Googled him and came up with zip, zero, nada.

"Second. An old friend from Lampasas High School is running this spa. One of two spas owned by a corporation named SpaCo." I spell it out for him. "A privately held offshore corporation with an address in Grand Cayman.

"Anyway, SpaCo owns Cielo Azul and another spa, off Baja in the Gulf of California, called Ola Azul. That's all I could get off Google.

"Bet you still have a few 'connections' with your 'friends' in the business. Oh, and while you're at it, see what you can dig up on a woman named Selena Channing."

CHAPTER 8

IT'S LATE OCTOBER, and, while the mornings are crisp, by noon the temperature is just about perfect. The deep blue, cloudless sky framing Wheeler Peak creates a spectacular view. I stand for a while, taking in the beauty surrounding me. Maybe the next few days won't be so bad after all.

Angela is already seated beneath the forest green and white-striped umbrella shading our table on the side terrace of the lodge.

I settle in the chair across from her and am about to share my version of the vista when Angela's face folds into a scowl. "Guess you saw who the spa director is."

When I nod, she hurries on. "I can't believe it's that awful what's-her-face Devering."

"Nigella."

"Whatever. All I remember is what a goon her brother was. He used to blow up frogs with cherry bombs."

"I never heard that. To me, he seemed a little young for his age, and shy. Sort of a frail boy."

She sniffs. "Frail, my ass. You must not have heard the things they said about him."

When I raise my eyebrows in question, she says, "Okay, maybe the frogs were just rumors, but the one thing we both know for sure is the Deverings left Lampasas in the middle of the night when the savings and loan failed."

Her face crumples. The next words out of her mouth are confusing but welcome. "Let's go back to Houston—today."

I'd just taken a swig of my tea and suppress a choke. "You've got to be kidding. We only just got here."

There are tears at the edges of her eyes. "I know, I know. But when I called to make a reservation in August, I didn't realize that stuck-up bitch would be taking poor Duncan's hard-earned money."

I never thought I'd be making a case for staying since the day has been oozing by like lava. Still. "But, Angela, Duncan has dumped a bundle of do-re-mi to treat you and me to this week. If we leave now, I don't think he'll get his money back."

"That's not true. Is it?" Angela searches my face, her eyebrows raised in question.

"Why would I lie? I'd sell my right arm if I could get back to Houston today. I didn't want to come in the first place."

She's managed to stanch the spate of tears that often follows her outbursts. Instead, she shakes her head. "It's your boyfriend, isn't it?"

"Boyfriend?" That's pure Duncan. "What's with the attitude?"

Angela sniffs her big sister sniff. "Duncan doesn't like him."

"How could he? Duncan's barely said two words to the man. In fact, no one in the family has asked to meet him."

Angela lowers her head. I know that move. She's going to deliver bad news.

"Mom and Dad don't think much of him either. He wasn't at the wedding like he promised. Thank heavens Duncan didn't ask him to be a groomsman."

I jump on the defense. "Bill was damn lucky to get to Chicago at all. Besides, I didn't expect Duncan to ask a complete stranger—"

I bite my tongue again before I finish. No point in opening what might be an old wound. Duncan and I were once engaged. I broke it off when I met Bill Cotton.

Angela drones on. "And they were shocked when you two holed up in that hotel in Lake Forest for a week."

Angela has always exaggerated. Still, I remember the look in Dad's eyes when I announced Bill and I would be celebrating New Years' at the Deer Path Inn instead of returning to Houston.

My sister ignores me. "Frankly, I don't give a damn about what happened in Lake Forest. I have more pressing issues."

Her pout turns to tears. "I miss my men. I miss having Duncan call me Angie. Do you know he's the only one who's ever called me Angie? I always wanted a nickname like yours. But no one ever ... Oh, Allie, can't you help me get home?"

Angela has always made impetuous decisions and regretted them the minute she got her way.

How any woman could make plans, in advance, to spend time away from her firstborn was a puzzle to me. But she had whined and whined until Duncan finally gave in.

My basic urge is to strangle her scrawny neck, but, instead, I reach across the table to pat her hand. "You'll have to suffer through another night. Marva told me Nigella's flown down to Ola Azul and won't return until tomorrow. And don't expect any miracles. As far as I know, most spas don't refund, but, maybe, because she knows us, she'll let you come back at another date and use the remaining credit."

Angela sniffs. "Fat chance of that. Not after the way I treated her in high school."

I return to my cabin to find an e-mail from Bill. No mention of Talavera.

Nigel Devering, of Georgetown, Grand Cayman, owned one-third plus two percent of the shares, acting as managing partner until his death in a suspicious boating accident last year. His shares are now divided equally between his daughter, Nigella Devering, and a son, also named Nigel.

The other two investors are Saul Sussman and Barry Wilson, both of New York City. Sussman owns a lot of Harlem properties. Wilson has a string of private warehouses up and down the East Coast.

The New York investment banking firm Spurger, O'Bryen has already purchased Sussman's shares but Wilson is holding out for more money.

Devering's heirs don't want to sell. But, if the bank can get Wilson's shares, the sale will go through and on the bank's terms.

That was quick—a little too quick, now that I think about it. Besides, I'm furious with Bill. Not one word about where the hell he was. No "I love you and miss you so much I ache." No "I'm counting the days until you're in my arms again." Just the facts. Damn his eyes.

It's around three when I finally find Angela and Rebbie at the Sacred Pool.

A small sign at the entrance requests the guests to speak quietly to honor the spirits that inhabit the stream. The last sentence reads: "NO CELLS, PLEASE."

Whether the legend is true or not, conversations are conducted in whispers beneath gentle breezes also whispering through the tall ponderosa pines that circle the area.

The tranquillity is shattered when Selena Channing invades, yelling, "*Ándele, ándele,*" at a beleaguered spa attendant struggling along, lugging that ubiquitous leather briefcase.

Selena plops in the last vacant chaise, points to the space beside her, and barks, "*Aquí. Aquí.*"

After ordering an iced tea *con naranja,* she drags out her cell and punches in a number. "This is Selena Channing. Get my secretary."

Her directives are given at the top of her voice. "My current bid is the same as before, but they still refuse to take it. How are you coming with Wilson?"

There's lots of eye rolling and some shhs, but she pays no attention. Nothing seems to faze her.

"If you can get Wilson onboard, I can cut our offer in half. It'll serve them right for being so greedy."

I lean toward Rebbie and whisper, "I'm going on a hike. Want to come?"

Rebbie jumps up. "Great idea. How 'bout you, Angela?"

My sister gives us a wicked smile. "And miss this? Somebody's going to shut that bitch up before the week is out. And, if it happens today, I want a ringside seat."

It seems a little strange that Rebbie keeps checking her watch every five minutes or so. Not that I don't have that horrid habit myself, but she doesn't seem to be that time-oriented.

It takes a little over ten minutes to reach the Tierra Amarilla Trail.

Rebbie checks her watch for the fourth time and stops. "Far enough for me. But you go on ahead."

I shrug. "I don't need to go any farther. I'll come back with you."

It's obvious from the vehement shake of her head that she doesn't like my offer. "Oh, no. It's not even three thirty. You have plenty of time. Please go on. I know you want to mark this trail off your list."

I don't even hesitate. Rebbie isn't a fast walker, and I've had to hold back to stay in step with her. "If you don't mind, I think I will." I check my watch. "I might be able to work in Rincon, too, if I hurry."

The words are barely across my lips when Rebbie gives me a wide smile and a farewell salute, then turns and walks toward the main lodge.

Two trails down and three to go. I'm passing Rebbie's cabin when the door opens and Tex Bodine, the hunky trainer/baggage wrangler, steps out.

He sees me, frowns, and stops short, then recovers his smile and says, "I just delivered a bottle of vodka and some plastic cups to Miz Dalton and was coming to knock on your door with an invitation."

I don't care much for straight vodka. "Maybe later, okay?"

"You better tell her yourself." He gives me a knowing leer. "I can't afford to get in any trouble."

When he edges past me, I can smell alcohol on his breath.

I knock.

Through the door comes a muffled, "Back so soon?"

The door flies open to reveal Rebbie wearing nothing but a towel.

When she sees me, her expectant smile dies. "Oh, hi."

I peer over Rebbie's shoulder to see the vodka on the night-stand next to a very rumpled bed. "I just ran into Tex. He said you wanted to invite me for a drink."

"Oh? Uh … uh … well, yes, I suppose. If that's what he said."

Rebbie's not very good at lying. Her large brown eyes dart back and forth several times before she says, "I ... uh ... uh ... was just about to get in the shower."

"Me too." I give her my best smile. "Why don't we skip the drink tonight? But how about joining Angela and me for dinner?"

"Thanks. I'd like that a lot. See you in a few."

Rebbie shuts the door before I can reply.

CHAPTER 9

LAST NIGHT, despite Angela's vehement objections to my proposed plan, I invited Rebbie to join us for all our meals.

Angela waited until we got to my cabin and then unloaded. "I thought we were going to have some quality time together. Why on earth did you have to throw Miss Whatchamacallit from Atoka into the mix?"

I think back to Rebbie's sad admission that prompted my invitation: "I have an eighteen-year-old son going to OU next year. All the Tulsa Daltons go to OU. Except for me."

And how Rebbie's blue eyes glistened when she said, "Big Mama Dalton finally solved that problem, but it took the bitch almost nineteen years. Last homecoming, she introduced my husband to Miss Tulsa, a twenty-three-year-old long-legged bona fide OU graduate. The good news is that I'm cashing out with at least ten million."

"Oh, for Pete's sake, Angela, can't you be just a little compassionate? The woman is sad and lonely. All she wants is a couple of buddies."

Angela doesn't go down easy. "Then why don't you invite the whole damn dining room to join us?"

I've come to enjoy Rebbie's no-nonsense approach to the fate her ex-mother-in-law has dealt her. It sure beats Angela's pathetic self-absorption.

I guess I shouldn't be so hard on my sister. I've been absorbed myself—trying to reach Bill.

I finally gave up punching in his number at midnight, surrendering to a fitful sleep, only to awake at just past five this morning to begin the exercise again.

To my sister's delight, we are lunching alone today. At breakfast, Rebbie announced that she could only get time on the climbing wall at twelve thirty. So she will be having her lunch at the pool.

I'm searching for my book, buried at the bottom of the spa-issue forest green canvas tote with my name stenciled in white, when Angela murmurs, "Here comes trouble."

I rise to see Nigella Devering heading in our direction. She looks fabulous. A picture-perfect tout for the spa. Though she's wearing spa forest green, her outfit could easily be from Dior. A cropped, gabardine jacket with raised collar stops at the waist above straight-legged slacks.

"Allie Armington, how wonderful to see you."

She throws her arms wide, and I jump up to meet her hug.

She looks down at Angela who continues to read as the hellos are shared. "Angela, is that you? I didn't see your name on the list."

My sister gives Nigella a slender smile. "Bruce? Mrs. Duncan Bruce? I'm an old married lady now, with a brand-new baby boy. How are you, Nigella?"

The smile is instantaneous and wide, her response clipped and chirpy. "Absolutely over the top, thank you very much. But, now that I know who you are, I do have a proverbial bone to pick with you."

Nigella waves her forefinger in Angela's face. "A Mrs. Bruce missed her welcoming appointment with me on Monday morning. Naughty girl, you must still be the same old slugabed I remember from Lampasas. Always late for classes and never present at morning assembly."

Angela is about to make some retort when our food arrives, and she digs into her enchiladas.

Nigella turns to me. "Unfortunately, I had to miss my appointment with you, Allie. Business before pleasure, they say. Can you ever forgive me?"

The overheard conversation between the two women replays. Channing is here to buy the spas. And, from what I've learned, it's a hostile takeover.

Nigella's piping voice interrupts my thoughts. "May I join you for lunch? There's so much catching up to do."

Angela shoots me a murderous look as Nigella takes the place set for Rebbie and motions for the waitress.

"I'll have the iced rose hip tea and the fruit plate, with a dollop of yogurt and a very generous sprinkle of flaxseed."

After the waitress leaves, Nigella continues. "Now, as I recall, the spring our family left Lampasas, Angela was being tutored in history and math so she could graduate with our class."

She pauses, then throws a beaming smile in my direction. "And you had just won the high school junior division of the state golf tournament. How's that for memory?"

Angela rolls her eyes and resumes her attack on the green enchiladas.

"Amazing," I say. "I'd forgotten all about the golf tournament."

Nigella covers my hand with hers and says with sad eyes, "I'll never forget your kindness. Never."

She glances at my sister. "Some of those girls were so mean."

My cheeks heat. Back then, Angela had prided herself on making Nigella as uncomfortable as possible. She often bragged she was the only one who had the guts to blackball Nigella from the Lampasas Girls' Social Club. Of course, in light of what happened to the savings and loan the following year, everybody was positive Angela was clairvoyant.

Nigella turns to Angela. "And I suppose after all that tutoring, you finally *did* graduate?"

Angela answers slowly. "Oh, yes. Right on schedule. But, of course, you wouldn't know about that, would you?"

I stiffen as that tiny, telltale twitch at the corner of Angela's mouth signals coming trouble.

"I graduated the day after your father drained the money out of the savings and loan, and your family went on the lam."

Nigella pales and jumps to her feet. When she speaks, her words are taut. "I just remembered an appointment. Excuse me."

She whirls away, almost colliding with the waitress carrying her lunch, who manages a quick side step, then turns to follow her through the door into the dining room.

I wait until the conversations around us resume, then whisper, "Why?"

"Why what?"

"What was the point?"

Angela gives me a dark smile. "Oh, dear me, did I need one?"

CHAPTER 10

AT BREAKFAST THE FOLLOWING morning, Rebbie regales us with a detailed account of her experience on the climbing wall the day before.

"Tex is just great. Have you noticed his arms? Like rocks. He was helping me belay to the top and never even broke a sweat."

I remember Tex's hurried exit from Rebbie's cabin. "Gee, sounds like things might be getting serious."

Rebbie blushes and says, "Gotta go. Tex is going to spot me again, and the only opening he has is now."

She takes a few steps then turns. "I had to reschedule my massage for noon, but, if you want to hike this afternoon, I'd love to join you. I'll be waiting on my cabin porch a little after one."

It's almost two by the time Rebbie and I climb the Lágrima Del Sol to Tierra Amarilla Trail.

After a good fifteen minutes, we arrive at El Paseo De Cristobal. Though marked in blue, it's not the easiest pass to negotiate, but one with the most beautiful vistas.

Halfway through the pass, Rebbie stops at a beckoning bench and plops down. "Hauling those extra pounds up that last steep hill has just about done me in. You go on ahead. I'll be right behind you."

"I'll be happy to wait. I'm not trying for a record."

She holds up her hand. "Don't be silly. Go on and enjoy the view. I'll be right along."

From the encroaching undergrowth of chaparral, it's plain that the black diamond Abiquiu Trail is seldom used. Despite the grueling ten-minute vertical ascent, the payoff is worth the effort.

Before me lies a breathtaking panorama of spruce- and fir-clad mountainsides, interspersed with gushing waterfalls, and, in the distance, the highest peak in New Mexico.

I settle on the nearest bench, lean back, and close my eyes. The calls of the birds high in the trees, accompanied by the sigh of wind, almost make my "sentence" bearable.

Almost.

My main problem is with Bill.

I let out a long sigh to ease the dull ache at the bottom of my heart.

I have to admit that I'm really not ready to go home. Because when I do, I'll have to face the truth about us: unless Bill and I make some drastic changes in our relationship, our future will be over before it begins.

When I hear Rebbie's gasping heaves, I check my watch. I shake my head, hating that I'm so obsessed about the time. I'm positive, if I had been wearing a watch when I was born, I would have made a mental note of it.

"You didn't say anything about a black diamond trail," she manages to pant. "My heart's in overdrive. But this view is worth every damn step. Mount Wheeler has to be the foothill of heaven."

I make a mental note to take the Abiquiu Trail at least once more before I leave. Then I notice the date square on my watch and sigh. "Only four more days to go."

Rebbie drops on the bench beside me. "Guess it hasn't been that much fun for you."

I shrug. "To be frank, Angela dragged me to the spa against my will. I have a fiancé waiting for me in Houston, but this time away just may be the proverbial straw that puts an end to the relationship."

She gives me a gentle pat on my arm. "I'm really sorry to hear that. But, hey, things usually work out for the best in the long run."

"We'll see." It's suddenly too painful to talk about Bill so I change the subject. "How's it going with Tex?"

Rebbie lowers her head. "Is it that obvious?"

"Well, he was rushing away from your cabin the other evening just as I was getting back from my hike. And he's spending a lot of time spotting you on the climbing wall."

She looks up at me with wide dark eyes. "I guess you must think I'm nuts to fall for a guy named Elvis."

"Elvis? I thought his name was Tex."

"Elvis Aaron 'Tex' Bodine. His mother was crazy for Presley. Poor man picked the name 'Tex' as soon as he could talk." She gives me a broad grin. "And I'm crazy for Tex."

"Just be careful. Men like Tex don't always turn out to be what they seem."

I stare away, lost in thought, until Rebbie's snorting snore breaks the spell.

I jiggle her awake. "We'd better be heading back."

She groans. "Down can't be that bad. At least it beats the hell out of up."

At the first turn, Rebbie points to a weatherworn sign: SHORTCUT TO LOWER RANCHITOS. "Let's go that way. I'm running out of gas."

I pull the map from my pocket and look it over before showing it to Rebbie. "How do we know that sign is right? There's no such marking on here."

But Rebbie ignores me to rush ahead and disappear in the underbrush. When I finally catch up, she's leaning against a tree stump, gasping for breath. "Sorry. I've run out of breath again. Go on ahead. I'll be right along."

After several minutes, the overgrown trail opens into a small, canopied clearing, broken by golden shafts of sunlight trailing through ponderosa branches. When I stop to enjoy the beauty of it, I hear approaching footsteps.

Thinking that it must be Rebbie, I turn to greet her. Then I realize the noise is coming from the other direction.

Almost immediately, a young Latina, clad in Cielo Azul spa issue, stumbles into the clearing from the opposite side. She's groaning between her rapid breaths, and, after turning twice to look behind her, she lifts her hand and pants, "*Yo estoy muriendo. Ayúdeme, por favor, ayúdeme.*"

When her knees start to give way, I reach her just in time to catch and lower her to the ground.

After a few labored breaths, her head rolls to one side.

My stomach clenches as I feel for the carotid pulse. None. Her skin is like ice, yet beads of sweat cover her brow. Her pupils are pinpoint. Before placing my hand over her eyes to close them, I note the time of death: 2:40 p.m.

My next thoughts strike like thunderbolts. A Latina dead from a possible overdose ... Ola Azul so conveniently near the Baja coast ... the Talavera cartel has to be involved. Why else would Ramón fly all the way to New Mexico, when there are so many luxurious spas in California and Mexico from which to choose?

Behind me, I hear Rebbie's footsteps and rush to meet her.

"Hey," she pants, "maybe we should go back the way we came from. This is really tough."

I grab her shoulders. "There's a dead woman up ahead."

Rebbie's eyes widen in silent question. Then she takes a deep breath and lets it slowly out. "Okay. I'm cool."

When we reach the woman, Rebbie's voice comes trembling from behind. "What do you think happened?"

"She probably OD'd."

I check my watch. Only a few minutes have passed, but it seems like hours. "We need to report this right away to the front desk—or whoever's in charge."

"Yeah, okay," Rebbie pants. "I'm right behind you."

We've taken only a few steps down the trail when men's voices float from below.

I raise my hand, turn, and put a finger to my lips. Then I check for a place we can hide.

To the right—nothing. But to the left is a small opening in the undergrowth that looks large enough for the two of us to slide through so we can hide ourselves behind the trunk of a toppled ponderosa pine.

I pull Rebbie in behind me, then motion her to the ground. Once she's down, I join her to crouch against the far side of the trunk. Praying whoever it is won't see us.

We're just settled when a man says, "There she is. She didn't get that far after all."

A few seconds pass, then he mutters, "Damn it to hell, she's dead. Doc didn't give us an accurate count of the take. You don't suppose the bloody sod's skimming, do you?"

The second man's drawl is too distinctive to miss. "Hard to trust anybody around here these days. Rio Arriba County is drowning in drugs."

My heart caves, and I glance down at Rebbie, curled into a quivering ball, hands covering her ears. Maybe she won't recognize Tex's voice.

The familiar drawl continues. "This is a hell of a way to transport drugs. We can't afford to lose a mule on every trip."

"Quit your complaining. There are plenty more where she came from. If you'll help me carry her to the utility cart, I can get her back to Walking Rain and make the airport in plenty of time for wheels-up."

"What about the others?"

"Don't worry, Tole is taking care of them. Just concentrate on how much we'll make once this shit is cut and distributed. Millions. Now be a good bloke and grab her ankles."

After a few grunts and groans, the footsteps fade.

Rebbie starts to rise, but I pull her down. Her big brown eyes search mine as she whispers, "What was that about? I was so scared I covered my ears."

"They came after the body."

She's silent for a minute, then says, "I think I know who one of them was."

"Yeah, me too. Did the other voice seem familiar at all?"

"No. But I'd guess he was English or Australian."

"Yeah. I pretty much got the same impression." I pull Rebbie to her feet. "Let's get out of here."

She struggles through the foliage, then turns my way as I break onto the path. "What are we going to do?"

"I'm not exactly sure. But, the one thing I do know is, we have to keep our mouths shut until I figure what our next move is going to be."

CHAPTER 11

IT'S THREE THIRTY by the time we descend Lower Ranchitos Trail, reach Rebbie's cabin porch, and collapse into the two rocking chairs.

After Rebbie regains her breath, she says, "What do you suppose that woman was doing up there?"

"After what I overheard, my best guess is that she was a drug mule."

Rebbie rocks for a few minutes, then says, "I saw a movie about that a couple of years ago. Young girls practiced swallowing grapes, then switched to drug pellets.

"I just don't understand why anybody would take a chance like that. If one of those pellets ruptured—"

"And they do. We had several cases come across our desks when I was with the Harris County DA. The five thousand in cash these women get for each trip is probably more money than they've ever seen. Enough to buy a house."

Rebbie thinks for a moment, then her jaw drops. "Are you saying those women are unloading the drugs right here at the spa?"

My answer is a shrug. If Rebbie didn't hear the reference made to Walking Rain, I'm not going to bring it up.

CHAPTER 12

A DRAB LITTLE WOMAN in staff uniform is sitting behind the desk in Nigella's outer office. A bright new nameplate reads: "Judith Orcutt, Secretary."

Whenever the phone rings, the woman reaches for the receiver and gives a running monologue: "Judith-Orcutt-secretary-to-Miss-Devering-may-I-help-you?"

Her muted exchanges are conducted behind her right hand, while her head bobs with each word she speaks.

Behind the closed door, I hear Nigella. When her voice rises, nervous Judith Orcutt jumps from behind her desk and scurries to the door.

She listens, shakes her head, then gives me a tremulous smile. "I'm afraid it's going to be some time before you can see Miss Devering. She's on the phone with the law."

That's a relief. Someone else has beaten me to the draw. Maybe I won't have to get involved after all. "Is there some kind of trouble?"

Orcutt puts a hand to her mouth and sidles back to her desk. "Oh dear, I've said too much. Miss Devering has sworn me to silence."

The door to Nigella's office flies open, and she lurches into reception. When she sees me, she frowns. "What are you doing here?"

"I'd like a few minutes of your time—if it's convenient."

"Convenient? No, it's not convenient. Certainly not now."

She closes her eyes, massages her temples with her fingertips, then shakes her head. "I'm terribly sorry to be so rude, Allie dear, but, frankly, I'm at my wits' end."

"Is there something I can do to help?"

She looks both ways, then motions me into her office, closes the door, and points me to a chair.

Once I'm seated, she lets out an exasperated sigh and begins to pace back and forth. "That bitch. Nothing but trouble since the minute she arrived. It's bad enough that banking firm sent her to pay us a pittance for our SpaCo shares, but for it to end this way ..."

A creeping dread tells me Nigella isn't referring to the dead woman on the trail. "And what way is that?"

Nigella stops pacing and begins to wring her hands. "Selena Channing is dead as a post. She must have died while she was using the Pilates equipment."

Two women dead at almost the same time? What a strange coincidence—or is it? Realizing that the poor woman has enough trouble on her hands and the law is coming in minutes, I decide to keep my news of the Latina's death for them.

"I have a vague idea of what kind of equipment that is. How did she ...?"

She takes a deep breath. "I don't know. I'm not into Pilates. You might as well have a look before the sheriff gets here. It could take him a while because of the switchbacks."

Before I can protest, Nigella drags me past Miss Orcutt, issuing a terse, "We'll be right back, Judith. In the meantime, call the kitchen and have them send over a large carafe of coffee with sweetener, cream, and several mugs. It's going to be a long afternoon."

CHAPTER 13

I FOLLOW NIGELLA DOWN THE DARKENED HALLWAY of the women's spa. All the doors are closed. Treatments are in progress.

We stop not far from the entrance to the gym at a door marked "Pilates."

When Nigella looks both ways, then inserts the key in the lock, I put my hand on her arm. "We really shouldn't."

"Nonsense," she sniffs. "I still own this spa, and, until it no longer belongs to me, I'll do anything I damn well please."

The door swings inward to reveal a room with a small window above a double door that opens to the outside.

The light filtering through the window is dim, but not too dim for me to make out Selena Channing, ash blonde hair pulled back in a ponytail, lying face up on what looks like a massage table with steel framing above. A fleece-lined hanging strap surrounds each ankle. One arm dangles lifelessly off the bed toward the cement floor.

When Nigella starts across the threshold, I catch her arm. "Don't go in," I whisper. "This could be a crime scene."

Nigella gasps, brings her hand to her throat, then stammers, "W-what? Are you saying she was murdered?"

"Murder is certainly one consideration, but, before we go there, let's wait for the sheriff to take a look and make that pronouncement. Lock the door, and let's get out of here."

"All right. All right." Nigella shakes my hand away and closes the door.

CHAPTER 14

ONCE WE'RE BACK IN NIGELLA'S OFFICE, I realize that this is my real first chance to see it.

Like the rest of the spa's public rooms, it features a ceiling of *vigas* and *latillas*, white smooth-plastered walls—one featuring an R.C. Gorman landscape—and Saltillo tile floors dotted with bright Amerindian throw rugs.

Her desk sits in front of a sliding glass door that opens onto a patio. Beyond is the center courtyard of the spa complex. On the opposite wall, a large fireplace, crackling in invitation, is faced by a comfortable couch and two easy chairs. In the far corner, a small table is set for two.

Nigella interrupts my thoughts. "Even though I couldn't stand the mouthy bitch, Channing died on my watch. And, once news of her death becomes public, our new clients will bolt. Worse still, the minute this hits the telly, it will kill any chance Nigey and I have to save the spas."

When she starts to pace and wring her hands, I guide her to the nearest chair, pour a couple of mugs of coffee, and place one in her hands.

I settle in the adjoining chair. "How close did you get to the body?"

Nigella shakes her head. "I didn't touch her, but I'm sure she wasn't breathing. I stood there a few minutes, then I got out of there."

I reach out to touch her arm. "I'm sorry I brought up homicide. Maybe she died from natural causes like a stroke or a heart attack. Though she's awfully young to have that happen to her. Who found her?"

Nigella takes a sip of her coffee, then shrugs. "I'm not really sure. Tex Bodine came to tell me. He mentioned Marva Weston."

That's a surprise. The last thing I knew, Tex was helping to haul a dead body down Lower Ranchitos Trail. And that was less than an hour ago. "And when was that?"

"About thirty minutes ago. No, maybe it was later. I don't … I really can't say."

She slams down her mug and leaps out of the chair to circle behind her desk. Once there, she pulls a stack of large index cards from a tray on the side of her desk and flips through them.

"Channing wasn't scheduled for a Pilates session. She must have been using the equipment on her own. I hope to God our liability clause covers situations such as this. Everyone is so litigious these days."

Nigella slumps into the chair behind her desk and lets out a prolonged sigh. "What now?"

"We wait for the law. But you might put Tex Bodine and Marva Weston on notice. I'm pretty sure the sheriff will want to question them."

A few minutes later, the phone on Nigella's desk buzzes, and she walks to the door and ushers in Tex Bodine.

When he sees me, he says to Nigella, "Why is she here?"

She gives him a nervous smile. "Miss Armington is an old friend—and also an attorney. Coffee?"

He gives me a long hard stare before settling in the chair across from me. "Black. Thanks."

Nigella fills a mug, hands it to him, then says, "The sheriff is on his way."

I turn to him. "So, you discovered the body?"

He takes a sip before answering. "No. I just happened to be at the spa desk, rescheduling a guest for the climbing wall, when Marva came running into the lounge area. She wanted to make the report herself but was concerned about being late for her next client, so I offered to relay her news to Miss Devering."

Nigella goes to her desk and lifts the page of a large desk calendar. "Marva should be done with her final massage for the day just about now. I'll get her."

Once the door to the outer office closes, Tex and I play stare-down for a few seconds.

Then he says, "And what did Miss Devering say you were doing here?"

"First, I'm here as Nigella's friend, but I used to be with the Harris County DA in Houston."

"You're a DA?"

"The operative word is 'was.'"

Just then, the two women enter. Nigella offers a mug of coffee to Marva. "There you go, my dear. Pity you were the one to discover the body."

The masseuse plops in the chair next to Tex. "What's he doin' here?"

Nigella looks my way and I say, "Once the sheriff inspects Ms. Channing's body, he'll want to question the two of you."

Tex jumps up. "Question me? About what? All I did was give Miss Devering the news."

"And all I did was return a blanket to the closet in the Pilates studio." Marva slams down her mug, stands, and starts for the door.

Nigella blocks her way. "Where do you think you're going?"

"I'm goin' home since I'm done for the day."

Before I came to Nigella's office to report the death on the trail, I had stopped by my cabin to grab the purse off the top shelf, check the Beretta, and feel for the extra clip zipped in the side pocket.

Now I'm glad I did, as I rise to join Nigella, hoping my next words might add a little authority. "As an officer of the court, I must advise you of your rights."

Marva squints in my direction. It's like she's never seen me before, much less almost every inch of my body. "What rights? I told you all I did was get a blanket—"

"As an attorney it is my duty to advise you, and"—I glance over at Tex, sidling toward the door—"you, too, Mr. Bodine. If either of you leaves these premises before the sheriff arrives, you could be considered prime suspects."

Marva's mouth drops open as Tex blurts out, "Suspects? Nobody said anything about murder."

CHAPTER 15

TEX AND MARVA ARE HUDDLED, head to head, over the small table in the corner. No wonder. Two women are dead, and it seems that Tex is involved in both incidents. He reported one death, and, though he didn't witness the Latina's death, he certainly knows a lot more about it than I do.

The door opens, and Judith Orcutt motions two uniformed men into the office.

Nigella extends her hand to a lanky, crag-faced man in uniform. "Thank you for coming so quickly, Sheriff."

She turns to me and says, "This is Sheriff Oscar Hernandez. Sheriff Hernandez, my friend Allie Armington."

The man nods at me but concentrates on Nigella. "At your service, Miss Devering. This is my senior deputy, Ricardo Santana."

The title is a misnomer. Santana hardly qualifies as a senior anything, unless he's in high school.

Tall and slender, Santana's sandy hair and pale, freckled face contradict his Latin heritage. The senior deputy gives me a shy smile, then inadvertently bumps into the sheriff, who mutters a few words under his breath, takes Santana by the shoulders, and moves him a couple of feet away.

"If you remember, son, I don't like it very much when you crowd me. So, how about you keeping your distance? Okay?"

He turns to Nigella. "I've been paging Ed Akins ever since your call came into the office. He's the doc in town who's acting medical examiner. I finally located him in Valdez."

Hernandez chuckles. "Can't keep a rod out of that man's hands. Loves fishing the Rio Hondo this time of year. Anyway, he's about a half-hour behind. That heap of junk he calls a hearse won't go much over thirty-five on any kind of grade.

"Rick and I came up in an unmarked car so as not to disturb your guests. But is there some other way we can bring the ME's vehicle in? I told Akins that retro look doesn't fit in the Taos County motor pool, but, when the idiot offered to personally pay for a lime green 1961 Cadillac hearse off eBay, I couldn't pass up an opportunity like that—even if looking at it could scare the daylights out of you."

Nigella gives the sheriff a nervous laugh, the laugh I remember so well from high school days. It still seems more like a bray. Finally, she manages to chortle, "Well, since you put it that way, we certainly don't want to create any unpleasant surprises for our clients. There's a service road to the right, just inside the main entrance. It leads directly to the side of the spa area and can't be seen from the main lodge."

The sheriff looks down at his watch. "Akins should be showing up pretty soon unless the radiator boils over."

He turns toward the door. "Okay, let's see the body."

When Marva, Tex, and I stand, the sheriff stops, turns toward us and holds up a hand. "Just Miss Devering, the senior deputy, and me."

Nigella grabs his arm. "But, Sheriff, Miss Armington used to be an assistant district attorney in Houston."

He gives me a flickering smile. "Then I'm sure she knows the fewer people at a possible crime scene, the better."

Nigella draws herself to her fullest height. "Miss Armington has already been there."

When the sheriff swings my way, his eyebrows arched, I raise my hand in my defense. "I know the standard protocol, sir. We didn't enter the Pilates room."

CHAPTER 16

AFTER INSTRUCTING NIGELLA and me to remain in the hall, Hernandez and Santana pull on latex gloves and enter the Pilates room.

Hernandez gives the situation a cursory once-over, then turns to Nigella. "When did you find her?"

She puts her hand to her throat, takes a step back, and says, "Oh, I wasn't the one who discovered the body. Tex Bodine informed me of Ms. Channing's death and suggested that I call you immediately."

The sheriff pulls a spiral notepad from his pocket and checks an entry. "I see that the incoming call was recorded at around four. Is that correct?"

Nigella shrugs. "I suppose."

He gives the corpse a second glance. "Looks like it could be from natural causes. I don't see any unusual marks on the body." He motions his deputy to follow, then returns to the hall.

When Santana strips off his gloves before reaching to close the door, Hernandez barks, "Don't touch that doorknob, Rick. How many times do I have to tell you that you have to use those damn gloves all the time you're at a possible crime scene?"

He turns to me, covers the side of his mouth with one hand, and says, "Kid's my nephew. Suffers from Attention Deficit. But he's all I got. Named him my senior deputy so I could keep an eye on him." Then he directs his attention to Nigella. "Pardon me, Miss Devering. Where's the woman who found the body?"

"That would be Marva Weston."

"Okay, Rick. You escort Miss Devering and …?" When he glances my way, I shake my head. "If you don't mind, Sheriff, I need to give you some pertinent information."

Nigella stiffens. "Did I hear you say you have pertinent information, Allie? What kind of pertinent information, might I ask?"

As my mind races through a short list of barely plausible excuses, I give her the broadest smile I can muster and pick one she might buy. "I'm interested in the legal procedure concerning a body discovered out of its home state. It won't take but a second."

Once Senior Deputy Santana and Nigella disappear through the spa waiting room door, the sheriff says, "This better be good."

I blurt, "Oh, it's good. Good and official. As a practicing officer of the court, it's my duty to report a second death."

"What?"

"I witnessed a second death earlier this afternoon."

He studies me for a few seconds. "Nobody said anything about that to me."

"Nobody else knows. I was taking a shortcut from the Abiquiu Lookout to Lower Ranchitos Trail when a woman came stumbling toward me in severe distress. I think she said she was dying. Then she collapsed in my arms. I noted the time of death. 2:40."

"Are you sure? 2:40?"

"I'm positive. I distinctly remember looking at my watch. It's a bad habit I have. One I can't seem to break."

"Where's the body?"

I mentally cross my fingers. No point in telling the sheriff any more than I have to. "Still on the trail—I guess."

"And you're just telling me about it now?"

"Miss Devering was already involved with the Channing incident and mentioned that you were on your way. That's when I decided to report directly to you instead of involving her."

Hernandez nods. "You were right to do that. Poor woman has enough on her plate." He pulls out the spiral notepad. "Where exactly is this trail?"

I hesitate only a second. Too late to turn back now. Even though the sheriff will come up empty-handed, I have to keep it going.

"I'll have to get you a trail map. Describing won't do much good unless you look at the map while I explain how to get there. It's about a thirty-minute hike if you don't stop."

"I can't believe you left a dying woman up there on that trail by herself."

"Of course I didn't. As I told you, I checked her vitals. There was no heartbeat. Her pupils were pinpoints. She was clammy and very pale. Classic symptoms of a drug overdose. I saw a few ODs when I was with the Harris County DA."

I'm a second away from telling him about the conversation I overheard on the trail, and the possible connection with the Talavera family, when I notice his strange reaction. Or, rather, lack of it—not at all what I would expect from a lawman who's just been given this kind of news.

He should be hurrying to Nigella's office to summon more uniforms, or, at the very least, dispatching his nephew with some help to retrieve the body. Instead, he stands straight as a ramrod, barely taking a breath.

The stone growing at the bottom of my gut tells me I might have accidentally cornered a rattlesnake.

CHAPTER 17

AS THE SHERIFF AND I enter Nigella's office, Rick Santana springs to attention. "All present and accounted for, sir."

The sheriff points me to a chair, then moves to stand in front of the group.

"As you all know, we have had an unfortunate incident up here, and it's my job to find out just exactly what happened."

When Santana takes an "at ease" stance, the sheriff turns his way. "What in hell are you doing, Rick?"

I can almost see those wheels trying to turn. Finally, he murmurs, "Looking for a possible suspect?"

The sheriff gives him a pained look. "Not that. Not that. We don't even know if the woman was murdered or not. Besides, I'm in charge of this investigation.

"You're supposed to be showing Ed Akins where the body is, before anyone sees that awful vehicle and panics. Now get on with it."

The deputy reddens, then takes a step toward his chief and speaks in a low voice.

The sheriff nods, then quietly says, very slowly, "Return to the door marked Women's Spa. Check to be sure there's nobody in the hall before entering. Find the door marked Pilates. Remember to pull on the gloves before you open the door. Cross the room to open the double doors to the outside. Step through the doors. After removing your gloves, walk down to the main road and wait for Ed there."

As Santana, blush still in place, bumbles toward the door, Nigella says, "Coffee anyone? It's fresh."

Mugs are filled, sweetener and cream are passed, and spoons clink against china.

The sheriff inhales a large swig and sets down his mug. "Okay, now which one of you discovered the dead woman?"

Marva timidly raises her hand. "I did."

"And when was that?"

"A little after three. My three o'clock complained she was cold, and, since we store the extra blankets in the Pilates closet, I went to get one. And there she was."

"Pardon me? Did you say three? An hour before we were notified?"

"Yes, sir. I ... I was in a real big hurry. So I just ran in, grabbed a blanket, and shut the door. Then I went back to tend to my client."

"You left that woman in order to tend to your client?"

Marva blushes. She looks down at her hands folded in her lap. Finally she says, "I didn't know she was dead. I thought she was takin' a nap." She lets out a lengthy sigh. "Well ... actually, I didn't get that close."

"You didn't try to rouse her?"

"No, sir. We're told not to disturb a client if they're sleepin', and my client was waitin' ..."

"And when you finished with your ... ah ... client, you went to find Mr. Bodine?"

"No, sir. I set up for my four o'clock first, then I took the blanket back to the Pilates room. I was surprised to see Miz Channin' was still there. She looked very comfortable, even though her feet were hitched up in those furry stirrups and one hand was danglin' over the edge of the bed. So, I just figured she was still nappin'. Then I said, 'Excuse me, I'm just returnin' the blanket I borrowed.' But, when she didn't answer, I ran lickety-split to the spa desk."

The sheriff shakes his head as he makes some notes, then says, "Were you specifically looking for Mr. Bodine?"

Marva looks at Tex, who raises his eyes toward the ceiling. She takes a deep breath and slowly lets it out. "Not him in particular. Tex just happened to be standin' there."

"Do you recall what time that was?"

"Well, sir, the sessions are forty-five minutes. We have fifteen minutes to get rid of the dirty linen, and set the table up with fresh, and use the restroom.

"It was about five to four when I left my room because I knew I would be late if I didn't find someone at the spa desk."

Hernandez jots down a few more words. "Miss Devering tells me Mr. Bodine was the one who delivered the news to her. Why didn't you?"

Marva looks at the man like he's one of the dimmest bulbs in the chandelier. "I just told you why ... uh, sir. I was afraid I'd be late for my next client."

Sheriff Hernandez lets out a long breath. "Guess Akins will have to establish the time of death."

Marva raises her hand. "Pardon me, but Miz Channin' wasn't a very nice person. Maybe she made someone mad. I mean mad enough to ... you know."

Hernandez scowls. "Let's not jump to conclusions here. The woman could have had a stroke or a heart attack."

Santana throws open the door. "Akins is here. I pointed him down the side road to the spa."

The sheriff turns to face the group. "That's all for now. Please do not—I repeat—do not talk to anyone about this investigation. If the woman died of natural causes, all we have to do is ship her body home. But, if we find otherwise ..." He pauses, then says, "Further questioning is pending until we get the body to Taos and the doc has a closer look."

The telephone on Nigella's desk rings only once before she grabs the receiver and turns away to speak *sotto voce* to whoever is on the other end.

After she hangs up, she steps from around her desk and whispers something to the sheriff, who nods.

Once Nigella has disappeared through the door to the outer office, Tex stands. "May I have a word with you, Sheriff? In private?"

Hernandez nods, and the two step through the sliding door to the patio. Both men turn away as Tex begins talking. Several minutes later, Nigella returns, just as the two shake hands and nod agreement.

The sheriff and Tex reenter, and, while the trainer busies himself with securing the sliding door, Hernandez turns to Nigella. "I wonder if you could spare Mr. Bodine for a few hours? We're going to need another pair of strong arms to handle the corpse."

That's odd. There's the sheriff, Senior Deputy Santana, and the medical examiner. Any two of them could easily lift Channing's body onto the gurney. She was little more than a bag of bones. Why would the sheriff need a fourth person?

Nigella nods. "Of course, Sheriff. Any way we might be of help."

Bodine has just stepped past me when the sheriff says, "And, Miss Armington, would you mind coming along, too? There are still a few questions that need to be answered."

The sheriff must sense my reluctance because he says, "I need more information on that other matter we discussed a few minutes ago in the hallway. Okay?"

When I still don't make a move, he smiles. "Or, I can just run you in. Your choice."

Nigella steps in. "But, Sheriff, Miss Armington hasn't a thing to do with Ms. Channing's death."

"I'm aware of that." The smile is still in place but his eyes mean business. "I need to speak with Miss Armington concerning the legal matter she mentioned earlier. Don't worry. I'll have her back in time for dinner."

I lob one last, weak protest. "But my sister is expecting me."

Nigella pats my arm. "You go along, Allie. Don't worry about your sister. I can cover for you."

CHAPTER 18

AS IT TURNS OUT, Sheriff Hernandez, Senior Deputy Santana, and I are driving to Taos in the unmarked car.

Once Santana joins us in the cruiser, we wait several minutes before the lime green Cadillac hearse moves slowly past us, and then we follow it through the gate at the Cielo Azul kiosk.

I grab for a handle as the sheriff's car hurtles precariously down the switchbacks, the setting sun glaring through the dust accumulating on the windshield.

Finally, Hernandez lets out a few curses beneath his breath, and then grumbles, "Dammit. Between that dust and the glare, I can't see a dagnabbed thing. Akins has always fancied himself as some kinda Indy driver. I'm not going to eat his dust one more minute."

He brakes the car, waits until the hearse rounds the next switchback, then carefully negotiates the next two switchbacks before he speaks. "Okay now, Miss Armington, the reason I asked you to come along is because I need more information about that woman on the trail."

From his perch on the backseat, Santana leans into the space between us. "Pardon me, Uncle Oscar, but I don't know anything about a woman on the trail."

Hernandez looks at me. The shake of his head is almost imperceptible, but it's plain he realizes he's just broached a subject he didn't intend to discuss in front of his nephew.

"I don't think that it's necessary to fill you in right now, Rick. In fact, I have another very important assignment for you to handle."

"But, Uncle Oscar, as senior deputy, I need to know these things."

"But not this particular 'thing,' Rick. I said I was handling it."

When we reach Taos, the sheriff takes Paseo Del Pueblo Sur to Albright, turns left, then parks next to a group of low ochre-colored stucco buildings fronted by a sign that reads: "Taos County Courthouse."

The building is mostly silent, except for the clacking sound of computer keys coming from a room down the dimly lit hallway.

Santana follows us to the bottom of the stairs, and has his foot on the first step, when the sheriff stops and turns. "After you clear off your desk, Rick, you can go on home. And when you get there, how 'bout defrosting some of Aunt Mert's chile for dinner?"

Hernandez's nephew takes a couple of seconds to process his uncle's directive. "Don't you need me up there? You know ... as a witness?"

"Thanks for the offer, but I think I can question Miss Armington myself."

"But Bodine and I were going for a beer after—"

"After what, Rick? Bodine has some business to finish with me before he can go anywhere. Best you take a rain check."

I'm seated across from the sheriff, holding a steamy mug of freshly brewed coffee, which should be the perfect antidote for that pesky stone in my gut. Instead, that stone keeps growing.

As far as I can tell, the sheriff has made no effort to recover the body I supposedly left behind on the trail. To me, that means he must know Tex is involved.

"I still don't understand why I had to come along, Sheriff. There's no point in making a report. The woman was an illegal."

He studies me a second or two before answering. "If you say she was an illegal, I believe you. And, if you say she died of an overdose, then she died of an overdose. I just need to get a few facts for the record."

I curse myself for telling the sheriff about the Latina at all, but, at that point, I thought he was on the up-and-up. Now, after watching Bodine and the sheriff speak on the patio outside Nigella's office, I'd lay bets the two of them are in this together.

Just as Hernandez sets down his cup and leans back in his chair, we hear footsteps and the sheriff calls out, "That you, Bodine?"

Tex appears at the door dressed in a pair of stonewashed jeans, a good-looking Ralph Lauren sports jacket over a navy shirt, and expensive hand-tooled cowboy boots.

He's straining under the load of a bulging leather briefcase— Selena Channing's briefcase.

After wrestling the briefcase to one side of the sheriff's desk, he drops it to the floor, and says to Hernandez, "As I explained on the patio, Sheriff, this briefcase holds the key to the trafficking operation I mentioned."

The sheriff turns my way and says, "In case you're wondering, Miss Armington, Bodine here is a federal agent."

I don't even try to cover my disbelief. With his curly blond hair and bright, toothy grin, Tex Bodine is hardly the type I would take for an agent. Most feds tend to be nondescript so they can blend into the crowd.

"You say you're a federal agent? There are all kinds of federal agencies in the U.S.—housing, agriculture, lots of others. Do you have some identification?"

Tex sputters, "For Pete's sake. I'm not carrying credentials; I'm undercover."

"For who?"

"Look, you're going to have to take my word. I *am* a special agent." When I shrug his protests away, he puffs with importance, drops his voice, and says, "Okay. What would you say if I told you that, even though Ms. Channing was representing the investment group trying to buy SpaCo, our agency was informed that she was also closely tied to the Talaveras?"

Tex pulls a small notebook from his jacket pocket and flips through several pages before he smiles and looks up. "Ms. Channing's maiden name was Selena Maria Gibbs. She was married for a few months to—"

I gasp. Of course. Selena Maria Gibbs had the same eyes as her brother Ray. I will never forget those eyes. When Tex flips another page, I try to refocus on what he's saying.

"—a Ronald Channing who died in a freak boating accident last year."

Tex's broad grin is bracketed by two deep dimples. "Says here she was a cousin."

"Talavera's cousin?"

He reads a few more lines. "Looks like."

"And that's why you have her briefcase?"

Before Bodine can answer, there's the echo of a second set of approaching footsteps.

Hernandez rolls his eyes to the ceiling. "I knew he couldn't stay away. That you, Rick?"

"Yessir, it's me. Just wondering if"—Senior Deputy Santana eases into the doorway—"Bodine was done." He grins. "Hey there, Tex. I thought you and me were gonna knock back a few at the Adobe Bar."

Tex looks surprised at Santana's remark; then, after a few seconds, he smiles and shakes his head. "Looks like I won't have time tonight, good buddy. Sorry."

The sheriff stands. "Did I not tell you fifteen minutes ago to give Bodine a rain check? What part of that didn't you understand, son?"

"I was counting on you being done by now." Santana shifts from one foot to the other a couple of times, then mumbles, "But I guess you're not."

Hernandez makes every effort to cover his exasperation. "No, Rick, we are not done."

Santana flushes, then he gives Bodine a shy smile. "Okay, then. Guess I'll drift on home. Unless you need me?"

"No, son, as I told you a minute or so ago, we don't."

Hernandez moves from behind his desk to follow his nephew to the door, stares after him a few seconds, then says, "I'll be home in about an hour. Don't forget the chile, you hear?"

CHAPTER 19

WHEN THE DOOR DOWNSTAIRS slams shut, Bodine hunches forward in his chair, his jacket pulling back to reveal a holstered weapon.

"I'll get right to the point, Miss Armington. For months, the FBI, in cooperation with the DEA, has been tracking the activities of a large-scale heroin and cocaine trafficking operation from Mexico into the border states.

"DEA Operation Jump-Start stopped the traffic coming across land, but, in a matter of weeks, the Talavera cartel began running small planes below our radar.

"That was okay for a while, but the Talaveras got greedy and wanted to move more product faster, so they hooked up with Nigel Devering.

"My previous assignment was to monitor the drug trade in Rio Arriba County, most especially Española, which, for many years, has served as a key distribution point for incoming drugs.

"Last spring, I was reassigned to help the DEA on a certain project related to the sting. Coincidentally, one of my narcs, who's been working at Big Rock Casino, was running a blackjack table and heard Devering bragging about all the money he was going to make flying drugs in here from the Baja.

"Problem was, even though Devering had the means to get the drugs into our area and a place to process them, he hadn't found a distribution contact on this end.

"After I signed on as a trainer at the spa, my cohort and I met with Devering to finalize the distribution part of the operation."

Bodine checks his empty coffee cup. "Mind if I have another jolt, Sheriff?"

I turn to Bodine. "I'd sure like to know more about Channing."

Bodine shrugs. "So would we. Actually, we were surprised when Channing appeared on the scene last week, screaming some big hoo-ha about SpaCo and selling the spas.

"There was no evidence of any sale of the spas prior to her arrival last Sunday.

"Now we think she might have been hooked up with Nigel in the romance department and was using the spa sale as some sort of distraction."

The sheriff takes a swig of his coffee. "This is all new news to me. Frankly, Mr. Bodine, the first I heard about this adventure was when Miss Armington reported that a Latina had OD'd this afternoon. Then, later, outside Miss Devering's office, you were kind enough to identify yourself as an FBI agent and give me a sketchy outline of the operation."

"That's right," Bodine says. "When the sheriff told me that you saw a woman go down on the trail, I asked that he bring you along. Would you mind giving me a brief rundown?"

I stare at Bodine a few seconds, trying to figure out exactly what he's trying to pull. I know it was his voice I heard. And I remember every word Devering said to him. Just what is he trying to accomplish by playing dumb?

"The woman was a Latina." As if he didn't know. "And once I ascertained she was dead, I went for help. That's all."

After I drain my coffee, I stand. "Look, what does any of this have to do with me? To be practical, the woman on the trail was an illegal, which makes her death unfortunate and tragic. I just happened to witness that death because I'm serving out a 'life sentence' at the spa with my sister. I don't see why I had to come into Taos at all."

I pick up my purse and turn toward the sheriff. "I'd appreciate it very much if you could get me back to the spa in time for dinner."

The sheriff rises. "Got all you need, Bodine?"

"Guess so."

Tex stands, then glances at the briefcase. "All right if I leave this here and hitch a ride back to the spa with you two?"

The sheriff nods. "Fine by me. But let's get going, okay? I was hoping to get home before *Wheel of Fortune*."

Bodine takes a couple of steps along with us, then pauses. "You go on ahead to the car. I have to make a call. I'll join you in a few minutes."

When the sheriff grunts his dismay, Bodine says, "Don't worry, I won't be long. You'll make it in plenty of time to see that first spin."

After we cross the parking lot to Hernandez's cruiser, he opens the front passenger door for me, then walks around the front of the car to slide behind the wheel.

"Sorry about the inconvenience. Guess Bodine thought you might have more to say on the subject."

If the sheriff only knew what I knew—but I'm not saying another word until I can find out who the good guys are. "Not a problem. What do you suppose will happen next?"

"I have no idea. But, if I have my way, me and my men will go on about county business and leave the exotic stuff to Bodine and the rest of his team.

"In the last fifteen years, the drugs have gotten so bad, hardly a day goes by that we don't get into it one way or another.

"Thank the Lord I'll be through with all this in January. I got a little spread over in Eagle Nest. Nice cozy ranch—two woodburning fireplaces and enough acreage to cow-calf it enough to earn a little."

He nods his head and flashes me a satisfied smile. "Yeah, whoever wins the election next month can be my guest."

Minutes later, when the door behind me opens and slams shut, the sheriff starts the car, then heads for the parking lot exit.

After pulling onto Paseo Del Pueblo Sur and heading north, the sheriff says to nobody in particular, "It won't take long to get back up the mountain. Never does this time of night. Most of the traffic has disappeared by now."

I'm hardly listening. That stone is still at the bottom of my stomach and growing fast.

Nothing about this trip has made any sense. I can understand why Bodine might reveal information about a covert federal operation to the sheriff, but why would he include a complete stranger?

When the vehicle rolls to a stop at the traffic signal, I turn toward Sheriff Hernandez to say as much, but the words stick in my throat as a damp cloth with a cloying smell covers my nose.

The sheriff glances my way, does a double take, then yells, "Who the—? What in hell are you doing?"

My head is pinned against the headrest while a weapon is aimed across me at the sheriff.

It's no use. I can't hold my breath any longer. I take a huge gulp of air, and, as everything begins fading to black, I hear, "Turn left. Now."

CHAPTER 20

I JERK AWAKE, head reeling like a washer on spin cycle, mouth tasting like the bottom of a birdcage, and a crick in my neck that says I've been in the same position much too long.

I open one eye to check out my surroundings. Through the haze, I see that my bed is a stack of burlap sacks piled on top of several plastic palettes, shoved in the corner of some kind of shed.

My head hurts too much to retrieve my memory. My main thought is to focus on finding my purse. After checking the cramped space, it's plain that my purse is not in here.

I let out a discouraged sigh. I have no idea where I am. I don't have a weapon, ID, or money. I'm in trouble.

I wobble to my feet and lurch toward the door, just as airplane engines fire. The shed vibrates so violently, the once dim sunlight slipping through cracks between the boards now seems to fill the room.

Panicked that the plane might ram into the shed, I push on the door. When it doesn't budge, I slam my shoulder against it. Two more attempts, and I'm pitched into glare as a rush of sand and pebbles—backwash from a departing twin-engine Cessna—stings my face.

Through slitted eyes, I make out a wind sock and beacon in the distance and, next to the closest hangar, a portable toilet, which I make for as fast as my aching bladder will allow.

After pulling myself together as best I can, I exit to make a second visual sweep. Near the end of the most distant hangar, I see the sheriff's cruiser.

I race down the gravel path, round the corner, and stop dead in my tracks. Parked toward the back side of the hangar is that awful lime green 1961 Cadillac hearse and, standing next to it, Senior Deputy Santana and two other uniforms.

When one of the men sees me, he points my way.

Santana whirls and yells, "What the hell are you doing here?"

He heads my way, hand on his pistol grip.

As he nears, I see that he no longer resembles the green recruit I met the day before. Patchy stubble and tired lines at the edges of his eyes have aged him considerably.

When he speaks, his tone is gruff and professional. "What do you know about this?"

I shake my head to clear the cobwebs. That hearse can mean only one thing—there's been another murder. And, from his tone of voice, Santana somehow thinks I'm involved.

I take a deep breath to calm myself. "Know about what?"

CHAPTER 21

THE DEPUTY DOESN'T WASTE any time delivering the grim news: Sheriff Hernandez is dead. A single bullet to the heart. And Tex Bodine—the "fed"—is nowhere to be found.

Santana shoves me into the backseat of the cruiser and, with siren at full blast, whisks me back to his office.

Though the trip from the Taos Regional Airport to the now familiar group of ochre buildings on Albright Street doesn't take long, my brain is working at Mach 5.

Bottom line: if Bodine has disappeared, that makes me "it."

Santana points me to the same chair I sat in the afternoon before. Funny what one notices under duress. Those coffee mugs are still on the desk where the sheriff, Bodine, and I left them, but Channing's bulky briefcase is nowhere to be seen.

Santana takes his place behind the sheriff's desk, pulls several color photos out of the center drawer, and lines them up.

One is a close-up of the sheriff on the ground, face filled with blank surprise, arms thrown wide. A pair of handcuffs is clutched in his right fist.

I swallow hard to suppress the bitter bile that catapults to the back of my throat, then clear it a few times before I say, "I'm very sorry for your loss. Having to head this investigation must make it doubly hard for you."

"My Uncle Oscar ...," Santana's eyes accuse me as he croaks, "never had a chance to reach for his weapon."

I meet his stare head on. I'm innocent and have no reason to be afraid. "Were those cuffs his?"

Santana whirls the picture in his direction, studies it a few seconds, then shakes his head. "He used plastic bands. Said they weren't so bulky. Carried them in his hip pocket."

"Last night, as your uncle was taking Tex Bodine and me back to the spa, Bodine put a cloth loaded with something noxious over my nose and held it there until I passed out. And now he's missing. Shouldn't that make him the prime suspect?"

"This yours?" Santana reaches down, pulls up my purse, and places it on the desk.

"Where did you find it?"

"On the ground next to Uncle Oscar's body."

"Oh, c'mon. Isn't that just a little too convenient? I mean, think about it. Why would I kill the sheriff and leave my purse next to his body?"

Santana shrugs, takes out my wallet, and waves it in my direction. "I took the liberty of checking the contents."

He removes my driver's license and the gun permit. "Says here you own a Beretta Tomcat 3032." Then he pulls out the empty holster. "What did you do with your weapon after you shot my uncle?"

The man is an idiot, but not one to mess with in his current state of mind. I take a deep breath and slowly let it out. "I didn't kill your uncle. If I was getting rid of my weapon, don't you think I would dump the holster, too?"

"Maybe you were in too much of a hurry."

"I guess that's one way to look at it, but, as I just told you, I was rendered unconscious before we got to the airport."

"You're saying my uncle—the sheriff of Taos, New Mexico, and one of the most upstanding, law-abiding men I know ... knew ... knocked you out?"

"I've been trying to remember what happened the last few minutes before I passed out, but the details aren't too clear. After Bodine clamped the cloth over my nose, your uncle said something. I think Bodine might have had a weapon."

He laughs. "Bodine armed? Bodine is a physical trainer at a spa. That uniform he wears hardly has room to conceal a weapon."

I'm about to correct him when I realize he has no clue that Bodine is supposed to be a fed. "But don't you remember? Bodine wasn't wearing his uniform. He had changed clothes."

Santana shakes his head. "Not when I helped him and the doc load the gurney into the hearse. He was wearing his uniform. I'm positive about that because that's when I suggested we go to the Adobe for a beer and made some crack that Bodine's trainer's outfit was so skimpy it would almost be illegal to wear it outside the spa."

"Did you see the body?"

Santana frowns and shakes his head. "The body was already bagged."

"Who helped Akins bag her?"

"Bodine, I guess. Akins and Bodine were standing beside that reducing machine when I got back to the room."

"Wasn't Bodine supposed to be riding in the hearse?"

Santana shakes his head. "Guess so. I don't know for sure. As you might recall, I rode down with you and Uncle Oscar."

I go over the time I was in the sheriff's office. Bodine had arrived in jeans and a jacket and dragging Channing's briefcase.

But when the sheriff, Santana, and I left for Taos, we were right behind the hearse. There was no time for Bodine to change clothes and get the briefcase. So, how did he get to Taos if he didn't drive himself?

But that doesn't make any sense either. If Bodine was driving his own car, why did he ask the sheriff to give him a ride back to the spa?

I look at Santana. "Try to remember what Bodine was wearing in the sheriff's office when you came to get him."

We lock eyes until Santana's waver and break contact. "I don't recall what he was wearing here in the office. All I remember is talking to Uncle Oscar. And when I speak to Uncle Oscar, I'm to pay strict attention."

I let out a long sigh. "Look. Why don't we go over this from another perspective? Okay? Say I did manage to overcome your uncle by aiming my Beretta at him. He was bigger than I am, and, as I recall, quite fit for a man his age. All he would have had to do was grab hold of my arm and twist it."

I pause to let Santana absorb what I said. "And if I did shoot your uncle, why would I leave my purse next to his body, spend the night in a run-down shed only a few hundred yards from the murder scene, and then reveal myself to you and your men this morning?"

Santana doesn't answer my questions. Instead, he leans over the desk to gather the photographs and place them in the envelope.

My patience has run out. I can't stand not knowing my fate for another second. "Are you arresting me or not?"

He drops the envelope on the desk, straightens, and puts his hands on his hips. "Actually, I can hold you for twenty-four hours as a person of interest."

"That's true. But be sure you have enough reason to detain me. I'm feeling more and more litigious every minute I have to sit here."

Senior Deputy Santana isn't at all happy. After consulting with a couple of the other deputies, he allows as how he doesn't have enough evidence to detain me.

He's even polite enough to escort me personally up the tortuous switchbacks, and drop me at the entrance to the main lodge.

As I slide from the car he says, "By the way, we checked Uncle Oscar's unmarked car for any sign of a cloth or the 'noxious' substance you described. Nothing was discovered. You better stay put—or else."

When I assure him that I'll be stuck at the spa until Sunday, he shakes his head. "Don't count too much on that. When we find the murder weapon—and we will—I promise on my uncle's death that I will take great pleasure in personally escorting you to a cell in the Adult Detention Center."

CHAPTER 22

"OH ALLIE, I can't believe they think you're a murderer."
Angela throws her arms around my neck in a choking embrace.

"But I'm not—"

Then the grim realization dawns that, unless the senior
deputy and his merry band can turn up Tex Bodine, I *am* the
only suspect in a capital murder, and I'm going to need an
attorney.

I peer over my sister's shoulder to see Nigella's brow creased
in an anxious frown as she murmurs, "News of the incident was
all over the telly this morning."

Then she mouths, "But nothing about Channing."

I arch my eyebrows over Angela's chatter and mouth back,
"Nothing?"

Nigella shrugs, and then gives me a "thumbs up."

Angela drags me into the spa director's office with Nigella
close on our heels. "What happened? I want to hear everything."

"Hold on a minute, okay?" I gently disengage myself and
step away from my frantic sibling. "I'll be happy to tell you everything I know, which isn't very much, but first I have to speak to
Duncan—in private."

"But I'm your own flesh and blood."

"I don't think you realize how serious this is, Angela. As of now, I'm the prime suspect in a capital murder. It's imperative that I speak to Duncan, attorney to attorney."

Nigella rises and points to the phone on her desk. "Remember to press nine for an outside line."

She turns to my sister. "This way."

Angela stands. "I'm not going anywhere with you."

Nigella ignores her. "How about a pastry and a cup of green tea?"

Angela's mouth drops for a small instant, then she rises to her full height. "After all the bad history we've shared, are you actually inviting me to share food with you?"

Nigella nods and gives me a sympathetic smile. "Your sister's been through a horrific ordeal. Let's try to make life a little easier for her by at least trying to be civil to one another."

Then she pushes Angela through the door and closes it behind her.

When Duncan answers, I don't waste time with pleasantries, and I omit the two women's deaths since neither seems to be of major importance in my case.

"The senior deputy thinks I shot the beloved local sheriff, who was his uncle and only relative. The man wants my hide. I need a good criminal attorney and quick. Please tell me you know someone around here?"

"What have you told them?"

"Nothing. But, Duncan, I ran into Ramón Talavera. Here at the spa."

"You mean"—I hear him swallow—"that Talavera?"

"Yes, dammit. There's something big going on up here. I don't quite know all the details, but I'm going to find out.

"And there's another suspect named Tex Bodine. He claims to be a fed, but I'm pretty sure he's the one who put the rag over my nose and knocked me out."

Duncan clears his throat a couple of times, which means he's thinking. "Surely the situation can't be as bad as you say. If I remember, you do tend to exaggerate."

"No, Duncan, Angela is the one who exaggerates. Listen to me. Bodine has disappeared, and this Santana I'm dealing with is barely old enough to shave.

"As far as I can tell, he doesn't have a clue why his uncle was killed. On top of that, the idiot thinks Tex Bodine is a fitness trainer at the spa and his best buddy.

"But Bodine claimed to be an FBI agent working with the DEA until he knocked me out."

"Good heavens, Allie, calm down. Are you on a secure line?"

I peer at the telephone. There are several other buttons that are either lit or blinking. "I guess."

Duncan lets out an exasperated sigh. "Damn you and your cockamamie stunts. What is it with you? Why is it you always seem to get yourself into such bizarre situations? And why must you always drag Angie in on your ludicrous adventures?"

That does it. I'm fighting for my life and my ex-fiancé has gone petty on me.

"You supercilious prick. How I ever thought you were the one I wanted to spend the rest of my life with is beyond me."

I take a deep breath then say, "In case you've forgotten, it was *your* wife who dragged me kicking and screaming out here."

There's a long pause as pages flip. Then Duncan finally says, "Actually, I do know a fine criminal defense lawyer in Albuquerque. Name's Clayton Bradford. I met him at an ABA seminar a few years ago. We shared a few drinks, told a few tales, and have traded Christmas cards."

Damn him. He's a past master at laying on the guilt. In my meekest, most conciliatory voice, I say, "Will you call him? Please?"

"Don't get your hopes up. He's a very busy man."

———

When the call from Duncan comes midafternoon, I'm dead asleep.

"You're on," Duncan shouts in my ear. "We'll be at the spa first thing tomorrow morning. Lucky for you we caught Bradford between trials."

"Did I hear you right? We? What is this 'we' stuff?"

"I'm flying in tonight and following Clay to the spa. I'll introduce you two, liberate Angie, and be back in Albuquerque in plenty of time to make the two o'clock to Houston."

CHAPTER 23

AFTER A LONG, HOT shower, I head for Rebbie Dalton's cabin. I have to knock several times before she finally opens the door.

"You?"

I step inside and shut the door behind me. "Gee, I expected something a little friendlier, good buddy."

Rebbie makes a halfhearted attempt at a welcoming hug. "But I am glad to see you. Are you okay?"

"I've had better days."

She waves to a newly opened quart of vodka and a stack of cups on the table. "I was just about to pour another drink. Care to join me?"

Over sips, I give Rebbie an edited version of what happened, excluding Channing's demise since her death hasn't been made public.

At that I give an involuntary shiver. If Channing really was a Talavera, that's a good enough reason why her death wasn't publicized. If it had been, it would have made great fodder for Tabloid-Land, and all it would take was one nosy reporter to jump at a story about a New Yorker visiting a local spa found dead on a Pilates table. Then, after a little more research, the connection to the Talaveras would be uncovered and revealed.

While Rebbie's chatter floats over me, I run through the press coverage of the very recent past. The local paper carried plenty of news about Sheriff Hernandez. Local football hero. Led the high school team to the state championship. Beloved community figure. Wanted to be a lawman all his life.

But not a word about Bodine gone missing, nor a peep devoted to what happened at the spa. Bodine, Channing, and the Latina—never mentioned. Big bucks have been spent to keep those names out of the news. Only a wealthy cartel like the Talaveras's can pass that much *mordida* around to quiet the media.

Rebbie's voice intrudes. "You look like you could use another splash."

I nod, hold out my cup, and continue telling Rebbie what happened the night before. How Bodine had chloroformed me, and then, when I finally came to that next morning, how the senior deputy had said he couldn't find Bodine, so he ran me in as the main suspect in the sheriff's death.

Rebbie pales when I tell her Tex has disappeared. It's then I decide not to mention his supposed connection to the FBI.

Frankly, after what that bastard did to me, Tex's seeming association with any kind of federal agency seems more far-fetched than ever.

During my spiel, I notice that Rebbie keeps glancing toward the bathroom door.

When she tosses down her drink and pours another, I say, "Is something wrong?"

Her response is just a little too quick. "Not a thing, except for your saying that Tex did you harm. That doesn't sound like the man I know."

"You think I made it all up?"

"Oh, no. No. I believe you—I guess. It's just that this news about Tex's disappearance is extremely upsetting."

It's then I realize Tex hasn't "disappeared" at all. He's stashed in Rebbie's bathroom.

All I have to do is open that door, and I'll be off the hook. That's all I have to do.

I'm just short of rising from my chair when those red flags begin to wave. What good would it do to expose Tex now? He must have risked a lot to come back to the spa to see Rebbie.

Besides, he's bigger and stronger than I am, and is bound to be armed. And, despite Rebbie's protestations of love for this man, if I exposed him, she could be put at risk as well.

I go over my times with Rebbie, mostly lunches and dinners before that ill-fated hike. And just when did we decide to take that hike? Didn't she suggest it?

And wasn't it Rebbie who pointed to the shortcut sign? In fact, it was she who insisted we go back to the spa that way.

I remember her racing ahead of me, then dropping behind as soon as we got into the underbrush.

I study my new-best-friend with renewed interest. Rebbie Dalton, the cute little divorcee from Tulsa, just might not be at all what she seems.

After deciding to make them both sweat a little, I let out my breath, lean back in my chair, and hold out my empty cup.

"Gee, that hit the spot. How about one more for the road?"

CHAPTER 24

IT'S A LITTLE BEFORE NINE the following morning when a very attractive man, preceded by Angela and Duncan, moves toward me across the main lobby of the spa.

His slender, sinewy frame is well over six foot. Iron gray close-cropped hair caps a high forehead. A long face features bright blue, intelligent eyes, an aquiline nose, and a generous mouth. He's the picture of power. Just the kind of man I want on my side.

He stands to one side while Angela and I say our good-byes, promising to keep in touch every day.

Duncan steps forward to peck my cheek. "We're running late. Good luck."

He turns to motion the man forward. "Allie, meet Clayton Bradford. Clay, this is my sister-in-law, Alice Armington, but her friends call her Allie."

"Miss Armington." Bradford grabs my hand in a steely grip as he gives me a long, careful once-over.

Seems I pass muster because he smiles, revealing an even set of sparkling white teeth, and gives an added squeeze before he releases my hand.

I motion him to follow me to a small conference room off the main lounge, usher him in, and then settle in one of the chairs at the table.

He folds his lanky frame into the one across from me, then pulls out a yellow legal pad and several sharpened pencils. After making a few notes, he looks up—all business.

"Apparently the law didn't possess enough evidence to book you, so at least we have that advantage."

"The law?" I hoot. "Just wait until you meet Senior Deputy Santana, and you'll drop that 'law' tag. This man is barely old enough to vote."

I give him a sad smile. "He's the sheriff's nephew and was devoted to the man. Hernandez told me he gave the poor kid that title so he could keep close watch on him. As far as I can tell, Senior Deputy Santana can barely fight his way out of a paper bag."

Bradford smiles back. "We'll deal with him when the time comes. How about starting from the beginning?"

While he takes copious notes, I run through the high points, beginning with the dying Latina on the trail, Channing's body on the Pilates, the executed sheriff, and the missing "federal agent."

After I finish, Bradford scans the pages crammed with his broad scrawl, then says, "Three people dead and one missing in less than twenty-four hours, and you're somehow involved with each?"

"I guess you could say that."

"You went back to the spa to report the Latina's OD, and that's when you found out that Miss Channing was also dead?"

"Yes. But there were a couple of things I didn't share with Sheriff Hernandez, nor Tex Bodine, and certainly not Senior Deputy Santana.

"The most important piece of information is—"

I glance toward the open door, then rise to close it. "Do you know anything about the Talavera cartel?"

"Only what I've read and heard in the news. That they're one of the most powerful crime families in Mexico."

"You got it. So, what would you say if I told you I ran into Ramón Talavera right here at this spa last Monday?"

Bradford stops writing and looks up. "How do you know it was him?"

"I had the 'pleasure' of meeting him once, several years ago. To brag on myself just a bit, I was the one who provided the government with the evidence that sent Talavera's cousin Raymond Gibbs to prison."

Bradford looks at me for a few seconds. "You sent his cousin to prison?"

"It's a long story."

"But it could be important."

"Whether it is or not, I'm more interested in the now. Don't you think it's strange that Ramón would visit this particular spa, 'at least once a month' as I was told, when there are far more luxurious spas located only a stone's throw from his home?

"And what about this? Bodine told the sheriff and me that Channing's maiden name was Selena Maria Gibbs. That makes her Ray Gibbs's sister. Bodine also intimated that she might be romantically involved with Nigel."

I pause to remember the Ray Gibbs I sent to prison. He could have been late forties or early fifties. It was hard to tell because he had snow white hair and looked like Santa Claus. To the best of my recall, he never mentioned a sister.

"That makes her Ramón Talavera's first cousin. She has to be involved on some level, don't you think?"

Bradford nods and jots down a short note.

"As I mentioned earlier, Channing arrived on the scene the same day my sister Angela and I did. She made a point of advertising that her New York investment firm was buying out the spas."

I shut my eyes, trying to recall more details.

"She had a huge leather briefcase that she carted wherever she went. Bodine brought that briefcase to the sheriff's office on Wednesday, saying it was the key to the sting operation the DEA was running. But, as far as I know, no one has seen it since."

Bradford studies me for a few seconds. "What about Nigel's sister? Is she part of this?"

I think back to the discussion I overheard while I was waiting for the appointment with Nigella.

"I overheard a conversation between Nigella and Channing, but something doesn't quite add up about that. If Channing were romantically involved with Nigel, why would she be threatening his sister?

"Still, Nigella has been nothing but kind and supportive, and she's done nothing that makes me suspicious of her. Bottom line, I honestly don't believe Nigella has a clue what's going on."

Bradford raises his hand. "Okay then, let's get back to Bodine for a second. You said he told you about the trafficking scheme?"

I nod. "That was really strange. If he really is a fed, I can understand why he might give that information to the sheriff, but why would he tell a complete stranger?"

Bradford makes a quick scan of his notes, then looks up. "I think I've got enough here for a little face time with Santana."

"Lotsa luck on that one. The guy has no clue what he's doing, or what is going on right under his nose."

Bradford stands. "I've taken the liberty of reserving a room for you in town. Much easier than my having to crawl up and down this mountain every few hours."

"But my bill is paid up here. No need to—"

As he jams the legal pad into his briefcase, he says very slowly and precisely, "I'm surprised you fail to recognize the gravity of the charges against you, Miss Armington. I'm sure you are well aware that the murder of a law officer is a capital offense. Since you and this Bodine are the only suspects, and Bodine is missing, I suggest you do what I say."

He doesn't look at me when he makes that statement. It's obvious he expects me to comply.

My first thought is to show some spunk—let him know I have a mind of my own. But his reference to "capital offense" tells me I'm in deep trouble and should keep any sort of snippy retort to myself.

I stand. "I'll get the rest of my things and change into my travel outfit."

He nods. "If I were you, I'd clear everything out. Just in case you won't be returning."

The look on his face is not very hopeful.

CHAPTER 25

WE MAKE A BRIEF DETOUR to the Taos County Airport to check out the shed where I spent Thursday night and take a peek at the sheriff's murder site.

It's well after three when Clay Bradford and I meet with Santana. The poor kid is aging by the second. In spite of a fresh uniform and the fact that he's managed a relatively nick-free shave, he looks worse than something the cat urped up.

Bradford introduces himself, and Santana acknowledges me with a curt nod, then motions us to sit.

"There's no way Miss Armington could have killed the sheriff," Bradford says. "She tells me she was rendered unconscious before she was left in that ramshackle shed at the airport."

Santana lets out a long sigh. "I have to admit that was somewhat of a puzzle in the beginning, but—"

He smiles and speaks like he's been studying the procedure manual all night. "Early this morning, a Beretta 3032 was found in the weeds behind one of the other hangars at the airport. One bullet was expended from the magazine, and there is a pretty clear set of prints on the grip."

Bradford leans forward, then turns my way, eyebrows arched. "Then you *are* saying Miss Armington was armed?"

Before Santana can answer, I say, "I'm licensed to carry a concealed weapon. And I had it stowed in my purse when I was with the sheriff and Bodine."

Santana turns to Bradford. "I personally witnessed Miss Armington in the company of my uncle and Mr. Bodine not one hour before the ME's specified time of my uncle's death."

He pauses and looks toward the ceiling until whatever he was searching for pops back into his brain. "Oh, yeah. We'll need a set of Miss Armington's prints."

"No need," I say. "They're already in the system. I was printed when I got the permit for my Beretta."

Santana slowly shakes his head. "That's real nice, but this is a small operation we have here. We haven't gone high tech yet."

While I assault the incriminating ink stains on my fingertips with a sanitary wipe, I say to Santana, "I'm sure I've been set up."

His eyebrows go north. "Yeah? By who?"

I shake my head. He knows so little, and what could he do about it anyway? Bodine is missing, and there's no one at the spa I can finger.

"What I mean is: what's the point in running a ballistics test? We both know what the results will show. This whole procedure is an unnecessary waste of time."

"You let me be the judge of that, okay? We're doing this one by the book because I want that noose around your neck to be nice and tight and legal."

A shiver traces down my spine. Santana means business, even if he is only a boy.

Then the senior deputy proudly announces that he's put a special rush on the forensics.

Bradford makes a good case for not throwing me in the slammer until they find Bodine, or unearth more proof against me, then assures Santana I will not be a flight risk.

Santana confers with someone down the hall, returns, and reluctantly agrees to let me go, asking us to be back at the courthouse by four the following afternoon when the reports would be ready.

Bradford weighs in. "Speaking of that. I'd like to have a little chat with the ME."

Santana shakes his head. "Can't."

The attorney's chin juts out. "What do you mean by 'can't'?"

Santana gives him a slow, lazy smile. "Akins is off on his annual fly-fishing trip."

I gasp at that news. "He's gone on vacation with two bodies in the morgue?"

"Akins finished up last night and hauled off right after that." Santana smiles at Bradford. "He usually starts in the Wild Rivers Area, then goes on up north to Colorado. He'll be gone a couple of weeks at least."

Bradford stands and motions for me to do the same. "Would it be possible to see the sheriff's body?"

"What for?"

"First to pay my respects. Your uncle seems to have been a fine person. And, second, to see the face of the man my client is supposed to have killed."

Santana lets out a long breath. "Since there's no official morgue in town, we use Cantu-Hume Funeral Home. Turn left off Albright on Paseo Del Pueblo Sur. It's two blocks down on the right."

"What about Channing?"

"Can't help you there, either. They shipped her body back to New York City yesterday."

CHAPTER 26

IT'S ALMOST SIX when Bradford and I leave the courthouse complex.

When he turns right on Paseo Del Pueblo Sur instead of left, I say, "I thought you wanted to see the sheriff's body."

He smiles. "As far as I'm concerned, you and I have put in enough time with the law. We both deserve a drink.

"Besides, Channing's body is already in New York, and, from what I hear, the sheriff's not going anywhere soon. The service is on Monday."

After taking a right on Kit Carson Road and traveling past several adobe buildings, Bradford turns left at 317 to pull beneath the porte cochère of a tan, Pueblo-type, two-story building.

A bellman steps forward to remove our bags from the trunk as the doorman helps me from the car, saying, "Welcome to El Monte Sagrado."

Bradford registers for both of us, directs the bellman to take me to my room, then says, "See you in the bar. How does seven sound?"

The Anaconda Bar is jumping by the time Bradford and I settle at a table, which, on closer scrutiny, turns out to be a large version of an Indian tom-tom.

When he gives me an approving once-over, I feel the beginnings of a blush and break eye contact to study the bronze-scaled underbelly of a large snake winding across the ceiling.

Bradford hails a waitress. "I'm ordering. What'll it be?"

"Chardonnay. By the glass is fine."

"Nonsense." He scans the list and says to the woman, "We'll have a bottle of the Stag's Leap Chardonnay and two glasses, but I'll start with a Ketel One on the rocks, with a spritz of vermouth and several olives."

After the cocktail waitress leaves, Bradford pulls out his notes and scans them before he begins his interrogation. "Tell me more about this Selena Channing."

I begin with the noisy ride from Albuquerque to the spa and my encounters with her over the next few days, adding that she had her briefcase by her side most of the time.

I follow that with Channing's screaming conversation at the pool. Then I say, "Do you think the briefcase was filled with cash to buy out the Deverings?"

Bradford shrugs. "Probably not actual cash. Treasuries maybe. Whoever possesses them, owns them."

"Maybe Bodine left town with the briefcase."

"Could be." Bradford adds a few sentences to his notes, then smiles across the tom-tom. "I guess the best approach is to suspect everybody—except you—since you're my client and claim to be innocent."

Once we've been served, Bradford settles back to take a taste of the Ketel One while I try the chardonnay.

After a couple of sips, he sets his glass down and leans forward. "After what you've told me about the Talaveras, it seems pretty obvious that someone from the family has set you up. Any particular reason come to mind?"

"When I spotted Ramón in the gym last Monday morning, I think he was surprised to see me there. But he was very gracious—

even when he mentioned that his cousin was in the federal prison at Madrid.

"To my relief, Talavera said he was leaving that day, and I assume he and his wife did just that."

I pause, then say, "But we have to consider a very important point. No one could have predicted that I would witness what happened last Thursday on the trail. If I hadn't gone hiking and stumbled onto that poor woman, they would have disposed of the evidence without any trouble. I'm a witness to a crime—a Talavera crime."

Bradford gives me a solemn nod. "That's very true. But think back. Was the sheriff the only one you told about the Latina?"

"Yes. But he was the one who told Bodine."

"And that was when Bodine told the sheriff he was a fed?"

I shrug.

"Could the sheriff have told anyone else?"

"Not that I know of. I was with him from the time we left Miss Devering's office until that cloth was clamped over my nose."

"The bad news for you is: the clip in that Beretta has one bullet missing, so we have to assume it was used on Hernandez."

"But not by me. Someone had to have commandeered my weapon."

"And when do you think that happened?"

"After I was rendered unconscious. Certainly not before then."

Bradford takes another slug of Ketel One, then says, "Didn't you say there was some sort of disagreement between the sheriff and Bodine just before you passed out?"

"I've gone over those last moments again and again, but all I can come up with is buzz instead of words."

"Too bad. Maybe it will come to you later."

I let out a discouraged sigh. "Let's hope."

Bradford ticks off a check on his list. "So, tell me, who is this Bill Cotton?"

He waits for my answer, and, when none comes, he raises his eyes to meet mine. "Duncan tells me this Cotton used to be with the Drug Enforcement Administration."

I nod. "He was. But he recently resigned. We were planning to get married and then set up a law practice in Houston."

I sigh and look away, knowing that I have to face the nagging doubt that Bill Cotton hasn't left the DEA. That would explain how he got the information on SpaCo so quickly.

Bradford and I spend the next few minutes in silence. He seems to be waiting for me to say something, but I see no need to help him along.

Finally he leans forward and says, "Not much of a Chatty Cathy, are you?"

I give him a slow smile. "No."

He thrums his fingers on the arm of his chair for a few seconds, then says, "I know all about you. Had you researched before I agreed to take your case. Scratch golfer. Texas Law Review. Harris County DA. Perkins, Travis. Quite a résumé."

He waits for my reply, piercing blue eyes boring through mine.

When none comes, he says, "Don't you want to know anything about me?"

Of course I do. The man is a hunk. A *single*, brilliant hunk. Instead, I give him an indifferent shrug. "I know all I need to know."

There's a frustrated snort, followed by, "This is possibly the worst conversation I've ever conducted with a member of the opposite sex."

"Sorry."

He lets out a disgruntled sigh and takes another sip of his martini.

Finally, I take pity on him and lean forward. "Okay, in the interest of time, maybe I should tell you what I do know. You were born and raised in Goliad—"

He gives me a triumphant smirk. "Wrong, right off the bat. Gonzales."

"Okay, Gonzales. Give me a break; both towns begin with G. After you got a ROTC scholarship to A&M, you put yourself through law school at the University of Houston by working nights at a car repair garage.

"You moved to Albuquerque after law school because your first wife grew up there. The marriage lasted five months after you passed the New Mexico bar.

"Over the years, you've earned quite a reputation for never losing a case—even if your client is guilty."

He gives me a self-deprecating smile. "I wouldn't say that."

"What about the good-looking widow who shot her husband in the right buttock while he was running up the stairs? You claimed he was going to kill her with his graphite tennis racket, and she shot him in self-defense. I heard there wasn't a dry eye in the jury box."

A wrinkle creases his otherwise tautly smooth forehead, and he leans toward me. "You've got most of it right. I did move to Albuquerque because of Brenda, but she was the one who left the marriage—for Hollywood."

We both lean back in our chairs. While he downs his vodka and orders another, I take a sip of my chardonnay.

Strangely enough, I'm enjoying the give-and-take of the conversation. Usually this type of man, one so obviously sure of himself and so very much in control, is a turnoff, but, in Clayton Bradford, these traits seem more intriguing than annoying.

I wait until the waitress brings a second Ketel One and he tastes it.

"To continue. You're in your midforties, and you've been single for about five years. Your second marriage lasted less than a year. No kids."

He smiles. "As I mentioned, Brenda left me for Hollywood. But, even I have to admit, Hollywood was the better choice. She's done very well. In fact, she's just signed to do a sitcom."

He takes another sip. "Jodie presented other problems. Too young, too greedy. Seems I lean toward picking the wrong types, but I'm working on that. And I do want kids, but I've got to meet the right woman first."

"Good luck."

"Yeah."

We sit staring at each other for a few seconds, then Bradford says, "Guess we've about covered all the essentials."

He stands and extends a hand. "That makes dinner the next item on our agenda."

CHAPTER 27

THE TELEPHONE DRAGS me out of semiconsciousness, and Clay Bradford's voice booms, "Are you planning to snore the whole day away?"

I squint at my watch. Ten o'clock already.

"Sorry, I haven't slept very much over the last few days. What's up?"

His voice lowers. "I have some very interesting news. How quickly can you meet me in the dining room?"

"An hour."

"Not sooner?"

One hour and fifteen minutes later, Clay Bradford—in jeans, bulky black sweater, and matching turtleneck—is fidgeting in his chair, tapping the ubiquitous notepad with his pencil.

I put on a contrite expression and give him a conciliatory open-armed gesture. "Sorry. It took longer to get myself together than I expected."

He checks me over and jumps to his feet. "The wait was worth it. You look spectacular. Have a seat. Since it's late, I ordered from the brunch menu. Hope you don't mind."

Seeing the look of delight in his eyes causes my heartbeat to ratchet up a notch. I'm surprised by my reaction—pleasantly surprised.

When my eyes finally meet his, he gives me a half smile. "Cat got your tongue?"

I ignore his question. "You said you had something?"

"Yeah, I do. While you were playing Sleeping Beauty, I drove over to Cantu-Hume to view the sheriff. I say 'view' because he was already cosmeticized and suited up in his uniform."

"Poor man. Did you know he was planning to retire in January? He told me he had a place in Eagle Nest. From the way he spoke about it, it seemed he was really looking forward to getting out of this rat race."

Bradford shakes his head. "Too bad he didn't make it."

He drains the rest of his coffee as if to wash the unpleasantness away, then says, "I had a nice little chat with the young woman on duty. After thirty minutes or so, I casually mentioned that I had heard about a death at the spa.

"Seems the gal is Akins's niece. Sometimes he lets her sit in on his autopsies."

Bradford looks both ways, then leans forward. "When I asked if she sat in on the Channing autopsy, she looked real surprised, then told me that no autopsy was performed."

"Are you telling me Akins sent the body to New York without an autopsy?"

"Apparently. What does that mean to you?"

"Maybe the Talaveras stepped in to cover up foul play, or maybe ...?"

My mind dances from one end to the other, trying to retrieve a half-formed thought that stubbornly refuses to be shaped.

Finally I say, "Think about this for a minute: Channing is a Talavera. But why was she at the spa? Solely to get the Deverings's shares? And why would anyone want her dead? Killing her wouldn't stop the sale if that was what she was really there for. It would just delay it. It just doesn't add up."

He nods. "It's moot now, but you're right. It doesn't add up—at all.

"I made a few calls. The casket was received by a bald man in dark glasses, who drove a black Cadillac hearse. He had all the correct papers. No more info available. It's sort of like Channing dropped off the face of the earth."

"Yeah," I say. "No autopsy, no charges, no mention of a thing about Selena in the press. And—no body? Hmmmm."

He grabs his pen, jots a few lines, then says, "Not to change the subject, but there's no news on Bodine. I did a little checking with a couple of the agencies. They never heard of him."

My stomach squeezes. Less than twenty-four hours ago, Bodine was hardly ten feet away from me. I had my chance. I didn't take it. God knows where he is now.

"But, since Bodine has disappeared, I'm all Santana has."

"Don't panic. If Bodine is undercover, his agency has to protect him."

"But maybe he isn't a fed at all. Maybe he's part of the setup?"

"Yes, it could be that. But, let's pretend for the time being that Tex Bodine really is a good guy." Bradford reaches across the table to give my hand a reassuring grasp, sending a stream of pleasant shivers through my body.

My hand stays in his until Bradford finally breaks his eyes from mine, looks down, and pulls his hand away.

Two quiches and iced teas arrive.

Bradford shoves his tea to one side, asks for more coffee, takes a sip, and carefully sets the cup in the saucer.

He stares down for a few seconds, then finally begins to speak. "Don't you think it's time to bring Santana in the loop? He may be mentally challenged, but he is the law."

I phrase my answer with the same care Bradford has posed his question. "Under most circumstances, as an officer of the court, I would wholeheartedly agree.

"But what if Santana—even though I think he's too stupid to be deceitful—what if the Talaveras own him? If we let him think that we suspect something, wouldn't we lose what little advantage we have?"

CHAPTER 28

AT BRADFORD'S SUGGESTION, I rest in my room until three, then pack my meager stash of clothes and meet him downstairs in the lobby.

No need to discuss why he's asked me to pack. The way things are looking now, odds are I'll end up in a cell by dinner.

We exchange idle chatter until a waiter arrives with two glasses of wine.

Bradford clinks his glass against mine. "This is for good luck."

"Or to numb me for the trip to the pokey?"

He laughs, but it isn't very comforting.

After I take a sip of the wine, I ask the big question. "What are my chances? Give it to me straight. I need to know exactly what I'm up against."

Bradford leans forward. "I won't lie to you. Whether you like it or not, you're the main suspect in the sheriff's murder since you were last seen with Hernandez and Bodine.

"And you couldn't have a worse enemy than Santana. Especially since he's Hernandez's nephew, and the man who—whether he deserves it or not—holds the top position until the newly elected sheriff takes over in January.

"He may act like a greenhorn and a dolt, but don't underestimate him. He's out for blood—and, right now, that blood is yours.

"If the bullets and prints match, we'll have a very steep mountain to climb. That kind of hard evidence will be difficult to dispute. And, unfortunately, the only two persons who could corroborate your alibi are dead or missing."

Each word comes like a shot. Bradford has let me have it with both barrels, but I need to hear it. This is no longer a game.

As we drive in silence back to the sheriff's office on Albright Street, all I can think about is what Clayton Bradford can do to defend me against that damning bullet and the fingerprints I'm sure will match mine.

Then there's the grim truth about posting bail. None is considered in capital cases. Even a high-powered attorney like Bradford would have a hard time convincing a judge to let me stay out of jail until the trial. Worse still, the courts are bogged down with cases. I might not get out of New Mexico for months ... years ... maybe never.

CHAPTER 29

AS WE FILE INTO THE OFFICE, Santana rises. He doesn't look much better than he did the last time I saw him. His scraggly beard is mostly stubble, and deep circles underline his eyes.

He motions us to sit, then settles behind the desk and opens a folder. After reading a few sentences, he looks up and says, "It seems you're off the hook, Miss Armington." He pauses, then adds, "For now."

My jaw drops. Did I just hear Santana say I'm off the hook? I look at Bradford. His mouth is open, too.

The deputy drones on. "The lands and grooves of the bullet from your Beretta don't even closely resemble those on the bullet we took from my uncle's body."

Santana reads the entire report before he looks up again. "Not only that, but the fingerprints don't match. Actually, the prints are those of a male. We've sent them to Albuquerque. They're running a search through the system as we speak. And we have a BOLO out on Bodine. Sooo ..."

He pulls a manila envelope from a side drawer, removes my weapon, and shoves it in my direction. "Here's your 3032."

I look at Bradford again, then back at Santana. He gives me a dry smile. "You're free to go. Actually, you are free to leave the state. We'll get in touch with you if something new arises."

104 I LOUISE GAYLORD

Bradford stands, reaches his hand across the desk, grabs Santana's, and practically shakes the man off his feet. "Since you have nothing further to say, Senior Deputy Santana, my client and I will be delighted to be on our way."

Neither one of us speaks as we make our way down the stairs and out the door leading to the parking lot. I should be jumping up and down with joy. Instead, all I can think is that the exercise was too pat.

Bradford slowly puts the key in the ignition but doesn't fire the motor. He finally looks my way and says, "That was almost an out-of-body experience back there."

"Boy, you can say that again."

He starts the engine, backs out, then stops. "By the way, I guess congratulations are in order. Too bad I didn't get to strut my stuff. I thrive on cases with no apparent way out."

"If you don't mind, I'd just as soon you strut someplace else."

Bradford smiles. "Hey, I resent that."

He turns north on Paseo Del Pueblo Sur. "I'll be more than happy to drive you to Albuquerque, and you can be on your way back to Houston by late this afternoon."

"Thanks for the offer, but I just might spend another night or two at the spa."

Bradford swerves to the side of the road, jams on the brakes, and brings the car to a screeching stop. "You've got to be kidding."

"No, not at all. Channing's death has been shoved under the rug. Bodine has dropped out of sight. And I want to know why."

He gives me a puzzled stare. "I thought it was pretty obvious that Channing was killed to stop the sale."

"But her death doesn't make any sense at all in the general scheme of things—especially since she's a Talavera. It's just too fishy. Even if we could point a finger at Nigella, it doesn't make sense. If Channing and Nigel were an item, don't you think Nigella would know? I doubt she'd bump off Nigey's girl."

Bradford pulls out the legal pad and flips through the pages. "Channing wanted to purchase both spas. If, through her efforts, the Talavera family could legally acquire the properties, think what an advantage they would have."

I nod. "That's why things don't add up. There's something I'm missing. Something that keeps poking at the side of my mind, but I just can't seem to get at it."

"Do you think Tex Bodine could be legit?"

"After what he pulled, I'm inclined to say no."

"Okay then, what was Bodine doing with Channing's briefcase?"

I shrug. "He said it was the 'key' to the sting."

Bradford shakes his head. "Can't you just let the law handle this?"

"You met the law. What do you think?" I pause, then add, "Doesn't any of this interest you even a little bit?"

"I'm a criminal defense attorney, Allie, not an investigator."

Bradford stares ahead for a few seconds, then lases me with those bright blue eyes. "And, do I have to remind you that neither are you?"

I smile. "Actually, I'm seriously considering a career change. How does Allie Armington, PI, sound?"

When he laughs, I counter with, "You have to admit, I have quite a knack for investigation."

"If you mean you're too damn curious for your own good, I'll grant you that."

"So, it can't hurt to follow up on a few leads, can it?"

"Actually, Allie, it could hurt and hurt badly. Do I have to remind you that, until just a few minutes ago, you were the major suspect in a capital murder? And now, probably thanks to the generosity of Ramón Talavera, you've been given a free pass?

"If you'll remember back a few days, once you mentioned the Latina to the sheriff, he was killed, Bodine disappeared, and you were left as the only suspect. See how easily you were pulled into it? If it was that easy the first time, just think what the Talaveras might do if you don't get outta Dodge?"

We spar all the way up the mountain.

When Bradford pulls to a stop in front of the main lodge, he grabs my hand. I watch his eyes soften, then drop to look at my mouth for the briefest instant. If I'm reading him right, he's thinking about kissing me.

He must reconsider because he clears his throat and pronounces, "As your lawyer, I want it on record that I strongly object to your plan."

I'm as surprised at the abrupt change in Bradford's attitude as I am by the rush of disappointment that floods through me. Then I realize that I wanted him to kiss me.

"Duly noted, counselor." I struggle to take my hand from his, slide out of the car, and open the back door to grab my bags. "Thanks for the lift. I'll keep in touch. In fact, I added your number to my speed-dial list."

"Gee, I guess I should be honored." He takes a deep breath and lets it out. "Isn't there anything I can say to change your mind?"

"Nope."

CHAPTER 30

THE DOOR TO CABIN FOUR IS LOCKED. That's a surprise. Then I remember I was never given a key. None of us were. All the cabins had been unlocked, with lights on, and a warm fire crackling in the kiva fireplace to welcome us.

I leave my suitcase on the porch and hurry to the main desk.

"Hi there. I've been staying in Cabin Four, but I had to be away for a couple of days. May I have the key?"

The young woman smiles. "Name?"

"Armington, but it might be under Bruce. My sister's husband was footing the bill."

"Oh, yes. Here you are." She pulls out a card and scans the attached yellow sticky note. "This says to notify Miss Devering immediately if you should return. Certainly you must be aware that you are booked only through tonight."

"Yes, indeed. I do realize that I have only one night left, but, under the circumstances, I thought the spa might extend my stay for a few days."

She gives me a stony stare. "Just one minute, please."

Ignoring the phone at her elbow, she disappears into the back office.

After a muted conversation, she reappears.

"Miss Devering would like to speak with you. She's in her office."

Nigella, the scheduling book tucked under her arm, comes from behind her desk. She's not smiling. In fact, she looks plainly annoyed.

"I must say, I'm quite shocked to see that you've returned to Cielo Azul, Allie dear. I was sure that once you were cleared of the sheriff's murder, you would head straight for the airport."

"Actually, I considered doing just that very thing, but, since the last few days have been so stressful, I thought another week in this little bit of heaven just might be the medicine I need to put me right back on my feet."

Nigella stares at me a few seconds, then says softly, "But, as I recall quite distinctly, you told me you were bored to death."

"I know, I know, but then I discovered the trails. With an additional week, I think I can achieve my goal of hiking every blue and black diamond." I give her my best smile. "Think what an accomplishment that would be!"

She shrugs, then wheels away to lead me to the sitting area. After she points me to one of the easy chairs, she settles in the other to study the book.

"Cabin Four? Oh dear. We have someone coming in on Wednesday for Cabin Four." She bites her lower lip and taps her pencil.

"I'm very flexible. Surely there must be something else available."

"No." She looks up and gives me a sad shake of her head.

I give her a pouting sigh. "Well then, I'll take Cabin Four until Wednesday. And, who knows, maybe another accommodation will come up in the meantime."

The alarm on her face is almost comical. "Oh, Allie, my dear, you don't want to do that. We don't do rooms by the day. It's a week's commitment. And even though you're a dear, dear, friend, I simply can't make any exceptions to the rule."

"No problem. I'll be happy to pay the freight."

"But I'd hate to take your hard-earned money. Please, won't you reconsider?"

I shake my head. "My mind's made up. If it's all right with you, I'll take the cabin until Wednesday."

She lets out an exasperated sigh, goes to her desk, and picks up the telephone. "Please have Cabin Four opened for Miss Armington. She'll be along straight away."

Nigella walks me to the door. No good-bye kiss-kiss this time. Not even one of her tender pats. "Housekeeping will have the cabin opened for you by the time you get there. Have a pleasant evening."

CHAPTER 31

ONCE I'VE SHOWERED, I slip into a fresh warm-up and make my way to Rebbie's cabin.

When I knock, the door cracks just enough for her voice to trail through the opening.

"Oh—it's you. Hold on." Rebbie, her robe somewhat askew, opens the door. Beneath puffy lids, she stares at me through bloodshot eyes, then lowers her head and quickly turns for the half-empty vodka bottle on the table.

She splashes some in one cup, downs it, and pours again before she says, "Want some?"

When I nod, she hands me a half-filled cup, and we settle in the chairs on each side of the table.

Rebbie drains her drink while I take a sip and go over what I'm about to say.

"Want to tell me about Tex?"

"What?"

"You're not a very good liar, Rebbie. Guess you haven't had much practice, and that's a good thing."

"But, I—"

"Tex was here when I dropped by last Thursday. He was hiding in the bathroom."

"How do you know that?"

I smile. "Well, if you want to know how I figured it out, you kept looking at the bathroom door every other minute."

She smiles back and gives me one of her funny little shrugs. "Busted?"

"Yep. But, here's the problem. If the law finds out you've been harboring a man with a BOLO out on him—"

"What's a BOLO?"

"It's short for 'be on the lookout.' It's also referred to as an APB. But, look, it doesn't matter what the law calls it. The bottom line is that they are looking for Tex as hard as they can.

"The point I want to make as far as you're concerned is that you could be cited as an accomplice. Worst case scenario: if Tex is convicted of murder, you, as an accessory, could get up to five years."

I pause to let that sink in. "Do you really want to wait that long to enjoy Big Mama Dalton's money?"

Rebbie lets out a long sigh. "Tex did come back to my cabin."

"What do you mean by came back?"

She nods. "He came by right after you went to your cabin. That's when I asked—" She looks down for a second, then says, "That's when I asked him about the woman on the trail."

A cold shudder marches through me. "You told him we were up there?"

"Please don't hate me, Allie. But I had to know the truth."

"And what did he say?"

"He looked shocked. 'What woman?' he said. 'What are you talking about?'

"That's when I told him everything. But, Allie, he swore he wasn't anywhere near that trail. That he'd never even been on the trails. That he was in the gym with a client. He told me to check the spa schedule."

It's then the grim realization crowds forward. Tex knew all along I was lying.

But why, after Tex went to all that trouble to knock me senseless, did he leave me in that shed instead of finishing me off?

Maybe his only goal was to murder the sheriff, snatch the briefcase, and disappear.

I think back ... remember starting for the sheriff's car. Tex told us to go ahead, and he would be right down. He must have spoken with someone—maybe one of Ramón Tavalera's minions.

The scene in the car replays. This time there is no buzz. I remember the cool steel of the weapon against my cheek as the sheriff looks my way and yells, "Who the—? What in hell are you doing?"

I replay the scene. The sheriff said "who"—not "what."

Maybe it was someone the sheriff didn't know, and I just assumed it was Bodine because I expected him to get in the car.

Rebbie's sobs get my attention. "Oh, God, I didn't mean ... You have to believe me. I didn't mean for anybody to get hurt."

"It's too late for 'sorry.' The sheriff is dead."

I take a few seconds to calm myself before I continue. "You said Tex came back later? What time?"

"After midnight. He told me he was at the courthouse in Taos using the restroom, when somebody hit him from behind. And I believed him, because he had a huge goose egg on the back of his head."

"Did he tell you who hit him?"

She shakes her head. "Tex didn't say anything about anybody. He said he just needed to see me."

"Did he have Channing's briefcase with him?"

"Why would he have that woman's briefcase?"

I give an innocent shrug. "No reason, I guess. When did Tex leave?"

"Not until late the following night. I haven't heard a word from him since."

Rebbie lowers her head for a few seconds, then raises her tear-filled eyes to meet mine. "Tex is a good man, Allie. I know it in my heart."

"If he's such a good man, then he has nothing to fear by coming forward. So why hasn't he? And why did he disappear and let me take the fall?"

She looks down and sighs. "There's got to be a really good reason. I just don't know what it is. Tex and I love each other. He says he wants to marry me."

"If I were you, I wouldn't count much on that. Unless that man shows up and soon, he's probably wearing a very large black hat."

CHAPTER 32

AFTER A RESTLESS NIGHT of unsettling dreams, filled with snatches of unrelated conversations, I bolt upright in my bed, awakened by the picture of Marva and Tex huddled together, whispering, at the back of Nigella's office.

When the sheriff asked Marva if she had been specifically looking for Tex, I saw Marva glance at Tex, and I distinctly remember Tex gazing toward the ceiling. There has to be something between those two. But what?

There goes that something-poking-at-the-side-of-my-mind again.

When Marva discovered Channing's body, why didn't she report it immediately? No matter that a client was waiting on the table. And, later, when she found Tex at the spa desk, she asked him to tell Nigella.

Now Tex Bodine is missing. There has to be some connection.

It's a little after seven. As I stand beneath the soothing stream of water, a hazy plan begins to form.

I take breakfast alone since Rebbie begged off, saying she had a headache. My guess is vodka flu.

With my second cup of Jamaica Blue steaming in front of me, I pull out the Tuesday schedule. To my surprise, Helen, not Marva, will be giving me my massage. What on earth has happened to Marva?

I hurry down the path to the spa and Nigella's office. Orcutt, prim as ever, motions me past her station and into the office, where Nigella and I do the hello bit.

Then I say, "I'm scheduled to have a massage with Helen today. Is Marva all right?"

"Of course she is." Nigella flashes me one of her perkiest smiles. "Marva called in last Friday morning to request some time off, not that I blame her, poor dear. Discovering a dead body can't be much fun. And, since this week looked like it was going to be light, I said she didn't have to come in until Friday."

When she turns her attentions to the stack of cards in front of her, I start to leave.

Then I turn. "Since I'm going to be here for a few days longer, I thought it might be fun to run up to the ski area and have a look around. Are any of the spa vehicles available?"

Nigella gives me a disappointed look. "Unfortunately, no. The van is in Taos on a supply run, and the Navigator will soon be headed for the airport in Albuquerque."

She pauses, then smiles as she shoves a set of keys across the desk. "But why don't you take my car? It's in the employee car park. A black Mercedes coupé."

"Oh, I wouldn't feel right about that."

"Don't be ridiculous. I'd love to come along and show you a few birds common to the area. But, since we are shorthanded, life around here has become one big mare's nest. Exactly when do you plan to go?"

"I guess sometime after lunch. Can't miss a meal, you know."

It's ten o'clock when I slide onto Helen's table.

Twenty-five blessedly silent minutes into the massage her instruction—"It's time to turn over"—crawls through my haze. I can't believe it, but I've actually dozed off.

I flip, resettle, then murmur, "Sorry. Guess I fell asleep."

"Oh, don't apologize. That's the finest compliment a client can pay."

Helen seems to be in a good mood, so I say, "Where's Marva?"

"Miss Devering gave her a few days off. I think she had some time coming."

I take a long, deep breath. "Do you happen to have Marva's phone number?"

Helen works on my right shoulder for a few minutes before she answers. "We're not really that close. I don't see her too much away from the spa. I live in Arroyo Hondo, and she lives in Valdez with her son. It's a bright pink adobe. The only one in town. You can't miss it."

I think back to my first experience on Marva's table, and how she talked about her son who showed such promise in college but took the wrong path when he went to work in the casino down in Española.

I spend the next few minutes debating whether or not to ask the big question. Channing was murdered at the spa. And news travels fast, since people don't usually keep their mouths shut. At least not about a murder.

"Did you hear about Ms. Channing?"

Helen's hands are still only for a nearly imperceptible instant, and her response is barely audible. "Pardon?"

"She was found dead in the Pilates room."

Helen concentrates on my lumpy shoulder for a few minutes before she says, "I guess I did hear something about that."

"Can you tell me what you heard?"

She bends my arm behind my back and gives it a smart yank. "Maybe you should talk to Marva."

CHAPTER 33

REBBIE IS STILL SITTING AT OUR TABLE, but she has already finished lunch.

When she sees me, she jumps up and throws her arms around my neck—a real struggle for someone so short. "Oh, Allie, I was afraid I was going to miss saying good-bye."

That's a shock. Why is she leaving now with Bodine missing and a week left to go?

"But you can't go yet."

"Actually, I can. Miss Devering gave me a check for the full refund." She pulls a corporate check from her purse and waves it at me.

"But, what about Bodine …?"

Rebbie gives me a sly smile, reaches back into her purse, and produces a folded slip of paper, which she slides in my direction. "Look what I found on my bedside table when I came in from my last session on the wall."

The typewritten note reads: "Meet me at Taos County Airport at seven. Hangar Four. I'll be waiting. T."

Then her smile melts into a sappy grin. "Isn't Tex just the most romantic thing?"

I stare down at the note, and a kind of muted panic sets in as, somewhere at the side of my mind, red flags begin to wave.

"How do you know this is from Tex? It's typewritten. It could be from anyone."

"Of course it's from Tex. It's signed with a *T*. Know anybody else whose name begins with *T*?"

"It isn't signed, Rebbie. The *T* is typed."

I reach across the table to grab her hand as the words tumble forward. "Don't you remember? We heard Tex on the trail with Devering. They were there to get the Latina."

"But Tex said he wasn't on that trail, and I believe him." She pauses, then asks, "Did you actually see him, Allie?"

I think back. "No, I didn't, but—"

She shrugs and shakes her head. "Well, just maybe it wasn't Tex. Maybe it was someone who sounded just like him."

She sees the surprised look on my face and says, "Okay, okay, maybe it was Tex. But maybe Devering had a gun."

"Now you're grasping at straws."

She gives me a rueful smile. "I know you can't possibly begin to understand why I'm going to meet him, since you think he tried to harm you."

I think back to the seconds before I passed out. The sheriff had said "who," not "what." Maybe Rebbie's right. Maybe it wasn't Tex.

"Just be careful, because I've gotten sorta fond of you."

She shrugs and smiles, "Whatever."

"Whatever? You could be in danger. Don't you get it?"

"But you don't know that for sure, do you? I know it's been only a few days since I met Tex, but I think he's a good man—a man who wants to marry me."

"I hate to rain on your parade, but did you happen to mention Big Mama Dalton's money?"

"The money? Oh, for heaven's sake, I can't remember if I did or not."

I let out a sigh of defeat. Rebbie hasn't heard a word I've said.

She reaches across the table and pats my arm. "I know you're upset, but I've made up my mind. How about a farewell cocktail in my cabin a little before five?"

"Sure." I give in to the fact that anything else I say won't matter and manage to glue some sort of smile on my face. "I'll be there."

CHAPTER 34

AFTER LUNCH, I return to my cabin and check for messages on my cell.

Nothing.

Not one word from Bill since Monday. It's like he's dropped off the face of the earth.

I stow my cell and my Beretta 3032 in my backpack purse, and head for the employee parking lot tucked behind a stand of pines at the back of the spa building.

By the time I find Nigella's black Mercedes parked in a spot marked "Spa Director," I've formed a plan. I'll drop in on Marva, offer my concern, and do a little probing.

Helen was right. Valdez is so small that Marva's Day-Glo pink house is easy to spot.

I knock several times before the hot pink door cracks open and Marva's nose sticks out.

"What are you doin' here?"

The frown line between her eyes tells me she's not particularly glad to see me.

"Could I have a few minutes of your time?"

Marva shakes her head. "I don't rightly know if I should even be speakin' to you, since you threatened to have me arrested the other day."

"I didn't threaten you, Marva. I was trying to be of some help. After all, I'm an attorney. If you remember, I just said that if you left before the sheriff arrived, you could be considered the major suspect in Miss Channing's death. And I'm very sorry if I scared you. Actually, that's why I came—to apologize."

"Apologize? Words don't make things right, you know. It wasn't easy seein' that woman dead, and then to be threatened when I was just tryin' to do my duty. Besides, I was scared to death Miz Deverin' would fire me. Jobs are scarce as hens' teeth around here."

"I'm really sorry if I insulted you, Marva."

Marva winces a little before she says, "I thought we were friends."

"And we are. I've grown very fond of you the short time I've been here."

When I stick out my hand in an offer of friendship, she hesitates, then smiles as her hand meets mine. "You didn't have to come all this way to apologize. I don't bear grudges."

The door remains where it is. She's not inviting me in.

Finally she says, "Is that all?"

"Well, almost."

I take a deep breath and plunge ahead. "I was wondering if you might remember anything else about the afternoon Mrs. Channing died?"

"Like?"

"Oh, I don't know. Guess I'm just grasping at straws."

Marva gives me a suspicious look. "I can't tell you any more than what I told the sheriff, God rest his soul. I didn't go near the body. I just grabbed a blanket and ..."

Her eyes leave mine, and she stares down for a few seconds, then says, "I really shouldn't be talkin' about this—to anybody."

"Please, Marva, it's really important. If you remember anything unusual about that afternoon, anything at all ...?"

I pause to add a little drama. "My future as an attorney might depend on it."

"Why do you think I might know somethin'?"

I shrug. "I don't. Really. But I'm just a little more than desperate. It's quite possible you told the sheriff everything, but it would sure help if we could just run through that afternoon again."

She's clearly not buying, so I try another tack. "You see, even though I'm out on my own recognizance, things could go sour any minute."

She repeats "recognizance" to herself a couple of times, then, after looking both ways, pulls me inside and points to a bright pink Naugahyde love seat in front of a pink, kiva-style fireplace. The whole living room and connecting dining room give the impression of the interior of a huge fluff of cotton candy.

After we're settled, she says, "It was all over the television that they let you go. But, you know, the funny thing was, there was never any mention of Miz Channin'."

"Yes, I'm very aware of that. The senior deputy never mentioned Channing to the reporters. I can't help but wonder why.

"And, FYI, I'm still the major suspect in the sheriff's murder unless they can find Tex Bodine."

Her eyes widen. "Tex? What on earth does he have to do with anythin'?"

"Surely whoever reported the news must have said that Tex and I were the last people seen with the sheriff before he was found."

"Well, no. The reporter didn't mention a word about Tex. I woulda taken notice of that. Tex and my boy have been friends for a long time."

"Really?"

"They served in the National Guard back in the mid-1990s. People said they coulda been a pair of twins."

"Twins? My goodness. I bet that was fun for them."

"Aw, that's just what *some* people said. I couldn't see any resemblance at all except the boys were blond headed. Buster has always outweighed Tex by twenty or thirty pounds."

"Buster? That's your son's name?"

"That's what we call him. We baptized him Wesley Albert."

I park the information to one side of my brain. For some reason, it seems important that I do.

Marva flashes me a smile filled with pride. "In fact, it was me who recommended Tex for a trainer's job at the spa."

"That was so nice of you, Marva. I'm sure Tex appreciated your efforts."

"Well, to tell you the truth, I owed him. Tex was the one who got Buster off the hook when he got into a little scrape down in Española a couple of years ago. I sorta regard Tex as Buster's guardian angel." She gives me a broad smile. "My boy's been straight ever since that little brush with the law."

Boy, is that an about-face. Wasn't it only a few days ago she was telling me what a slug her son was?

Marva pauses to clear her throat a couple of times, then looks down at her hands.

I wait a few seconds, but when nothing else seems to be forth-coming, I add, "Unfortunately, Tex has disappeared. The senior deputy is looking for him."

I can see that Marva hasn't computed what I just said. Something seems to be distracting her.

She glances toward the dining room a couple of times before she shakes her head, lets out a sigh, then leans forward. "I like you, Miss Armington."

She moves so close I can feel her breath on my face. "So— maybe I do have a little somethin' that might help."

"Anything."

"Well," she mutters, "when I first went in the Pilates room to get the blanket, that Channin' woman was as alive as you and me. That's why I didn't report her death any earlier."

"Alive? Are you positive?"

"Sure as we're sittin' here. She called me a nosy bitch. Then she told me to get out before my boss came. That if my boss found me in the Pilates room, there would be plenty of trouble and I would lose my job."

"By 'boss,' do you think she meant Miss Devering?"

"I guess so. But since I was already runnin' late, I just grabbed the blanket and got out."

"But why didn't you tell that to the sheriff?"

"What was the point? The woman was dead when I went back."

"You're sure?"

Marva shrugs. "As sure as I could be. She didn't look my way or speak."

"But, Marva, maybe she was still alive."

Before Marva can answer, there's a slight noise behind us. So slight it might have gone unnoticed if Marva hadn't frozen for just an instant.

She looks past me, then jumps up and pulls me to my feet. "Thank you for comin' by and askin' how I'm doin'. As you can see, I'm just dandy. I'll be back at the spa by the end of next week. You can count on that."

At the front door, I pause and turn at the threshold, with every intention of making some sort of protest, but Marva shakes her head. From the look in her eyes, I decide I'd better do what she says.

Marva's street feeds into a cross street with a three-way stop. I honor the sign and turn right, intending to circle the block. It's then I see the "Dead End" sign.

I pull into the nearest driveway to turn around, just as a non-descript gray car screeches to a stop at the corner.

Marva is at the wheel. She looks both ways, guns the engine, and the car veers left. At the highway intersection, the car veers left again toward Taos.

By the time I make it to the highway, there's not a car in sight.

CHAPTER 35

IT'S JUST FIVE when I knock on Rebbie's cabin door. After several more attempts to rouse her, I turn the handle and step inside.

The single cabins at Cielo Azul are very similar. My accent color is brick red. Rebbie's spread was forest green. But it isn't now. It's navy.

Puzzled, I look around the room, then step back to check the number on the cabin door. Two. It's the right cabin. I step in the room a second time.

The rugs and spread have been changed. I walk to the bed, lift the navy coverlet to my nose and give it the sniff test. Brand-new.

I check the closet and drawers. All empty. In the bathroom, the spa supplies have been replaced. If I had a fingerprint kit and dusted for prints, I'm sure I would find none.

All the while the stone in my stomach has been growing. There's not one shred of evidence remaining to indicate that Rebbie Dalton ever occupied this cabin.

CHAPTER 36

THE RECEPTION DESK in the lobby outside the dining room is unmanned, but the seating areas around the fireplaces are filled with couples waiting for dinner.

I hurry to the spa to find that desk also unmanned. Not unusual for the end of the day.

To my relief, the door to Nigella's outer office is wide open. "Is she in?"

Judith Orcutt nods and points to the door.

I knock.

"Come?" Nigella looks up and smiles. "I was hoping you'd drop in because I have some very good news. With a little adjusting here and there, I've managed to stretch your stay until Friday. But that's the very best I can do. We're jammed from then until the Thanksgiving hols."

From the look on her face, I can tell she's expecting me to thank her. Instead, I blurt out, "Do you know where Rebbie Dalton is?"

"Goodness me, that's straight out of left field. Why on earth do you ask?"

"When I saw her at lunch, she made a date with me to join her for a drink in her cabin at five. I went. She wasn't there."

Nigella looks at her watch. "That's strange. Mrs. Dalton made arrangements this morning to leave right after lunch in order to catch the 4:40 American to Dallas."

"But she told me—" I stop in midsentence. Something is definitely wrong.

Nigella raises her eyebrows in question.

I say, "It was nothing. Really."

She gives me a sideways glance. "Mrs. Dalton must have told you something else or you wouldn't be here, would you?"

"All she said was to meet in her cabin for a drink at five."

"Well, my dear, I don't see how that could be possible since—"

She looks down, riffles through one of the ever-present stacks of file cards on her desk, and pulls a bright yellow card from close to the bottom of the stack.

She scans it, then smiles. "Here it is. The Navigator left here a little after one thirty. Mrs. Dalton was the only passenger."

CHAPTER 37

AT DINNER, I pick at the free-range chicken dish and share idle chatter at the open seating table. Two couples are visiting from Ola Azul. To hear them talk, it's an island paradise beyond compare. By the end of the meal, they've talked another couple into returning with them the following day. At least on the surface, Nigey's grand plan seems to be working out well.

On the way out of the dining room, I hear the hostess speaking to one of the wait people. "Did you hear about—?"

Her voice is overridden by a muffled crash from behind the closed kitchen doors. "It's all over the news. The hotels in town are overrun with reporters, and two news helicopters are up from Albuquerque. What is going on with this town? First the sheriff and now this."

I head for the coffee alcove. Several people are standing before the plasma screen, mouths agape.

Standing in front of the Cantu-Hume Funeral Home sign, a female reporter squints into the lights. "To repeat: At four thirty this afternoon, Dr. Edwin Akins, beloved local physician and acting medical examiner for Taos County, was found floating facedown in the Rio Grande River just south of the Wild and Scenic Rivers Recreation Area, his life ended by a stray hunting arrow.

"The two young men who discovered the body floating in a side eddy, said he was still clutching his prized Sage fishing rod.

"Dr. Michael Tole, who happened to be tenting in the Little Arsenic Springs Campground, reported that the arrow had entered the upper middle of Akins's back and continued through the torso to protrude from his chest.

"Though there is no conclusive evidence at this time, officials are deeming the death an accident."

The reporter waves over a man in a sheriff's department uniform. "Pardon me, Deputy? Did you work with Dr. Akins?"

"Yes, I did." He smiles into the camera. "Dr. Akins, besides being the acting medical examiner for Taos County, was an avid fly-fisherman and held many trophies for both salt- and fresh-water fishing."

She nods. "Thank you, Deputy. Can you tell us how this tragedy occurred?"

"Since it's bow season, we're guessing it was a stray arrow. Probably some bow hunter just got some place he shouldn't be."

The camera swings toward the right end of the building and its porte cochère, where the dreadful hearse is parked beneath the lights.

The reporter's voice says, "That's Dr. Akins's vehicle, a lime green 1961 Cadillac hearse that he personally purchased off eBay. We'll get back to you as this developing story unfolds."

It's after eight when I pass Rebbie's darkened cabin to enter mine.

I notice the next-day schedule is propped against my bedside lamp.

Monday
9   a.m.   Massage: Glenys
10   a.m.   Facial: Judith

| 11 | a.m. | Broth by the Pool |
| 1 | p.m. | Lunch |

Today your afternoon is free.

I put the schedule in the bath area so I won't forget it, then wander back into the bedroom and slump in the easy chair.

Where are you, Rebbie? Did you heed my warning and take the 4:40 flight back to Tulsa? Or did you meet Tex in that hangar at seven?

I stare at my cell several minutes before lifting it from its charger and punching the speed dial for Bill. When his message comes on, I hang up.

Clayton Bradford is next. Contacting him is the last thing I want to do, but people seem to be dropping around me like flies: first, the Latina woman, then Selena Channing, then the sheriff, and now Dr. Akins.

Tex Bodine is hunkered somewhere below the radar, Marva Weston was last seen racing west out of Valdez, and now Rebbie Dalton is God-knows-where.

I can't go to Santana. No one on the force can supersede his orders until the newly-elected sheriff takes office in January. It's not that the man is an obstructionist; it's just that he's woefully ill-equipped to handle much more than a flyswatter.

Two rings and Clayton's recording kicks in. He's out of town on a case. He gives several numbers and contacts to make in case of an emergency, then finishes with the promise to contact the caller by the end of five working days.

I hang up without leaving a message. What's the point? As Bradford said, he's a criminal attorney, not the law.

Sleep doesn't come easily. I try to read a paperback I bought at George Bush International, but what seemed like a good choice then, doesn't remotely hold my attention now.

It's well past eleven when I prowl my bathroom for a new bottle of water and, then, for the first time since I've been at Cielo Azul, I lock my cabin door.

CHAPTER 38

MY EYES FLY OPEN as a hand covers my mouth and a leg slides across my hips to pin me in place.

When the hand slips away to be replaced by a mouth, it's a mouth I know well. Bill's insistent tongue is tinged with that signature trace of salt, while his skin bears a hint of the aftershave that once made me go weak in the knees.

I drown in the intensity of his kiss. When he ends it with a still sensuous but less-demanding pull, he whispers, "God, I've missed you."

I turn on the bedside light. Bill is bare-chested, his lower torso beneath my coverlet.

"What in hell are you doing here?"

"I missed you. I had to come."

I know Bill much too well to believe that. Something far more important than missing me brings him to northern New Mexico.

He moves to kiss me again, but I shove him away.

"You're still with the DEA, aren't you? You moved out of my condo so you could work with them without arousing my suspicion."

Bill nuzzles my neck. "I was waiting for the right time to tell you ..."

"And the right time didn't present itself once during the last couple of weeks?"

"Please hear me out before you rush to judge, Allie."

He takes my hand in his as his eyes search mine. "When it was time to actually leave the DEA, I couldn't. The more I thought about sitting behind a desk dealing with other peoples' legal problems, the more it seemed like I would be serving out a life sentence at Leavenworth."

My stomach shreds in two as the rosy picture Bill painted the previous December as we lay entwined in bed at the Deer Path Inn crumbles to nothing. I shake my head, hoping to stop the words, but they keep coming.

"So, instead of handing in my resignation, I requested standby status with a six-month leave. Then they offered me a promotion I couldn't turn down—area agent in charge of the DEA's current operation. And, better yet, they wanted me to work out of Houston.

"I agreed before my superior could end his sentence. As far as I was concerned, I had struck a bonanza. I could continue the job I love and still be with you."

He brings his face close to mine to brush my lips with his. "The only reason I held off telling you for so long was because I was afraid when you found out that I hadn't exactly been up-front with you about this, you might want to end it."

I let a few seconds pass, then say, "Actually, I've spent most of the week trying to figure out what to do about us. Frankly, I dreaded returning to Houston because it meant I had to make a decision."

He lowers his eyes. "Then I wasn't too far off base, was I?"

I don't want to answer his question—at least, not yet—so I change the subject. "From what you've just told me, it seems you were already into this mess when you learned Angela and I were coming to Cielo Azul. Why didn't you say something then?"

"What could I say? The operation was—is—classified."

He searches my face for a second, then says, "But at this point, that's moot. When I learned that you were the major suspect in the local sheriff's murder, I got here as soon as I could."

"Who told you I was involved?"

"That's classified, too. Sorry."

"But I need to know."

Bill gives me his quirky smile as his finger zips across his lips. "No can do."

My next question—why didn't he answer my email about Ramón Talavera?—is at the ready, but Bill's lips meet mine. And those lips can be very persuasive when he puts his mind to it.

When we finally come up for air, Bill pushes away so he can see my face. "So, how did you get messed up in the sheriff's murder?"

I smile and shrug. "Looking back, I'm not exactly sure."

Again, that strange feeling resurges. Why can't I seem to trust a man I once so desperately wanted to spend the rest of my life with?

The story I relate is exactly what happened, except that I use "spa trainer" instead of Tex Bodine. I mention Santana only as the sheriff's nephew.

But when I mention Clayton Bradford's name, Bill's fingers tighten on my arms. "Who is he? And what have you told him?"

I instinctively pull back. The look on his face is not what I expect. His eyes are dark as night. His jaw is clenched.

"Duncan got him to defend me." I hesitate only a second before I make a decision. No point in mentioning my visit with Marva, or what I've realized is the possibility that Serena Channing might still be alive. "I told him everything I've told you."

When I try to pull away a second time, his eyes soften and he gives me that endearing grin. Then he crushes me to him. "I don't want to talk right now. There are far more important issues to address."

Bill turns out the light, then slides down beneath the bedding, pulling me with him.

I start to protest, but his lips find the side of my neck as his hand covers my breast.

CHAPTER 39

BILL AND I ARE SNUGGLED in "spoon position." The top of my head is nested beneath his chin, my shoulders are wrapped in the protective curve of his arms, and our bodies are molded together in all the right places.

I'm lost in dreamless sleep when Bill's warm blanket of a body hardens into ropy sinews.

His hand covers my mouth for a second time, and he whispers, "Someone's on the porch. Slide to the floor. Now."

Just as Bill settles next to me, my cabin door opens, and a muted release from a weapon equipped with a silencer is accompanied by a flash.

Neither of us breathes until the quickly retreating footsteps fade.

Bill rolls to his side and lets out a soft groan. "That was close. Too damn close."

The tile floor is unwelcomely cold against my body, and I scrunch into him, hoping to share his heat.

I murmur, "Whoever pulled the trigger couldn't possibly have made out much more than the outline of the bed. The curtains are closed."

Bill stands, pulling me up with him. He wraps me in the coverlet, then grabs the top sheet off the bed for himself and steps onto the porch. When he reenters, he says, "You're right. It's so dark in here I could barely see a thing."

He drops the sheet and steps into my coverlet, and I rest my head against his shoulder. I feel his heartbeat quicken, and tears sting my eyes.

I'm not surprised at his next words. "I want you to leave first thing tomorrow. That's an order."

He leans down, picks up a pair of spa warm-up pants from the floor, and pulls them on.

I slide my arms around his neck. "I know I should have gone back to Houston the minute Santana said I was off the hook. But I just couldn't. There's too much that's not right about the situation. Besides, you know how I am—too curious for my own good."

"That's the truth. You're too curious for everybody's good."

What a strange thing for him to say. "What do you mean by 'everybody'?"

He stares at me a few seconds, then takes me in his arms again. "I mean the two of us. We're everybody. Why do you feel something's wrong?"

I want to run down the list of the dead and missing but think better of it. A year ago, I wouldn't have hesitated to share my thoughts with Bill, but now …

"Nothing—I guess. I should have minded my own business and let the law muddle through this morass. But, now, after what just happened … well, someone must think I know too much."

Bill pulls me into him. "Don't say that. If someone wanted you dead, they would have fired more than once. My best guess is that the shot was just a scare tactic."

He kisses me, lets out a low moan, then kisses me again.

His next words are freighted with desire. "Do you know what standing this close to you does to me?"

Then he presses his erection against me in invitation.

At his touch, the flash of the gun and the whine of the silencer replay in my mind, and I jerk away, too shaken to respond.

His eyes harden only for a second, then melt to a twinkle in accompaniment to his quirky, lopsided smile.

"Guess you've got a lot more sense than I do."

He heads for the door, pauses, then turns. "If you need me, I'm in Cabin Ten."

When the door closes behind Bill, I turn on the light and cross the room to examine the bed. No sign of a bullet. Why am I not surprised?

I drag the comforter and a pillow to the arm chair, make myself as comfortable as I can, then toss and turn as I try to piece together the events of the last two hours. Something isn't right. Why is Bill here? He must have known I had been released. He always gets the facts first. He's been trained to do that.

When sleep finally comes, dawn has already lightened the sky.

CHAPTER 40

IT'S WELL PAST SIX THIRTY when I pull myself from my cramped accommodation to greet the day, and a little past seven when I reach to open the cabin door.

I jerk my hand away.

Last night, I had locked that door for the first time since I arrived at the spa.

I take one step back, followed by another, and then another, until I feel the mattress against the back of my leg.

Collapsing on the end of my bed, heart racing, I parse the details again and again, trying to get my mind around last night and what it means.

Bill and whoever fired that shot at my bed had to be working together.

It's then Bill's words replay: *"If someone wanted you dead, they would have fired more than once."*

A few days ago, somebody just wanted me out of the way. And, when I didn't disappear like a good little girl, it's obvious they decided to send in a bigger gun.

Bill has to be working with them.

Best case scenario: he's a double agent just doing his job.

Worst case … I try to shake the thought away. To even consider the possibility that Bill might have turned rogue is unbearable.

I think back to the first time I met Bill, and the intense jolt that accompanied his handshake as his electric blue eyes bored into mine. He was wearing the delicious, smoky aftershave that made my knees go weak. Did Talavera have Bill under his thumb that long ago? Or did Bill flip later, maybe when he stepped on the jet at Teterboro to fly his aged uncle to a safe haven in South America?

And what about the promises we made at the Deer Path Inn last New Year's? Did Bill know then he wouldn't be able to keep them?

Bottom line: whether Bill was here last night to protect me—or not—his motives are highly suspicious.

It was a blank, and Bill knew it.

CHAPTER 41

AFTER STOWING MY CELL, my Beretta, my cash and cards, and a trail map in my backpack, I exit my cabin.

But, instead of turning right toward the main lodge, I turn left to follow the well-groomed path that winds between the row of cabins and the roaring Cibolo Creek one hundred feet below.

The day promises to be another dazzler. Above the constant hum of the creek, birdsong fills the air, and the sun sparkles in dew-laden boughs. God may be in his heaven, but, as far as I'm concerned, absolutely nothing is right with my world.

As if things couldn't possibly get worse, Cabin Ten's roof has been taken down to the wood frame, and there are several ladders stowed along its side.

I step to the door and open it. The room is empty. Cabin Ten hasn't been occupied for days. If Bill isn't in Cabin Ten, then where did he go in his spa warm-up pants and bare feet?

Just past Cabin Ten looms a rock outcropping. The path crosses a narrow iron bridge hovering above the creek far below. At first glance, the way looks forbidding, but the railings seem sturdy and well above waist height.

No reason to turn back. Though I've never come this way before, the map shows this path looping around to join the Lower Ranchitos near the entrance to Walking Rain Retreat House.

I inch my way around the outcropping above the creek, then stop. Across the rushing waters, I can see yet another trail descending from the back of Walking Rain to the creek below.

Once across the bridge, I hurry along my path, then turn right where it meets the Lower Ranchitos.

Not a person in sight. I check my watch yet again. Seven thirty. It's still early. Most of the clients are breakfasting or using the gym.

The gate to Walking Rain Retreat House is unlocked. I walk up the path, then across the deep porch, dotted with conversation groupings of outdoor furniture.

At the living room end of the porch, a flight of stairs rises to the front porch on the second floor, but there doesn't seem to be a corresponding stair at the kitchen end. That's strange. Every other architectural feature of Walking Rain seems to be perfectly symmetrical.

Curiosity gets the best of me. I sidle past the French doors of the dining room, then by what must be the kitchen, to the end of the porch.

At this end of the house, practicality reigns. This is the loading area. There are several parking spaces and a wide turning apron. The door into the kitchen is an oversized sliding door with wide steps leading to it.

I follow the short, paved drive leading away from Walking Rain to the opening of a tunnel beneath Lágrima Del Sol Trail. No telling where it leads, but this must be the way they bring the drugs into and out of the spa.

My guess is, the road is below but parallel to the main road, avoiding the guardhouse kiosk at the entrance to the spa, then connects with the main road at some point.

Ten minutes have lapsed by the time I return to the building and swing open the front door into a sizable entry hall facing a wide staircase carpeted in a Navajo design.

To my left is a spacious living room with a large fireplace. The same interior design featured in the other Cielo Azul buildings is echoed in the Saltillo tile flooring and stucco walls.

The comfortable couches are in the same buttery leather as in the rest of the public rooms, and flanked by oak tables with keyed tenon accents and quadralinear posts.

To the right of the entry is the dining room. It features a classic Stickley Mission table, chairs for twelve, and a sideboard of the same design.

The next step is to check out the kitchen. Past the dining room, I slip through a swinging door to find a well-equipped commercial kitchen, complete with walk-in refrigerator.

And on the far wall sits a long metal table with six stools. To the untrained eye, it looks like a large prep area, but I've seen this type of table before—in a hangar in Mexico.

I have just grabbed the handle of the walk-in refrigerator when, from above, comes the muffled resonance of a familiar voice.

I'm halfway up the stairs when I hear an undeniable cadence.

On the second floor, to my right, is a small foyer-like indentation and a set of double doors. Behind those doors, I recognize Bill's voice. He's probably saying the same things to someone else that he said to me only hours before.

I'm frozen in place, wanting to run, but mesmerized by the slowly increasing rhythm on the other side of the wall. Then I hear Nigella Devering's signature bray.

I step away from the door, so numb my mind can't seem to make any sense of anything except ... Bill is having sex with Nigella Devering.

I want to beat down the door, scream his betrayal. And then ...

Instead, realizing that the two on the other side of the door will be occupied for a while longer, I take a few deep breaths to calm down.

I un-holster my Beretta 3032, tip up the barrel to see a round in the chamber, then ease across the hall at the top of the stairs and open the first door on the right.

The room is empty. It's almost a monk's cell. Two cots, a pillow and blanket for each, and a desk with one chair.

The only "windows" in the room are French doors that open onto the wide porch.

Who would pay a premium rate to stay in a sterile place like this?

I peek into the small, white-tile bathroom. A toilet and sink sit beneath a tiny high window. The long wall backdrops a low tub set a few inches in front of it. At each end, a handheld shower with attached hoses is mounted on the wall above its own drain. Two plastic seats, each with a hole in the middle, fit loosely over the edges of the tub to slide in either direction.

It doesn't take much to size up the situation. This is where the drugs are "delivered."

I think back to what Tex said to the sheriff and me. Something about Nigel delivering and processing the product, and Tex and his buddy distributing it.

A door opens, and I check my watch. Almost eight. I hear Nigella say, "I'll be back in plenty of time. Nigey promises they should be arriving around eleven."

Bill's muted question doesn't carry but Nigella's response does. "Don't worry. Tole and his wife will be here to supervise the delivery and weighing. Just make sure the men are in place."

Then the door shuts, and I hear Nigella descend the stairs and exit the front door.

My first impulse is to rush into the suite and confront Bill in order to end whatever he thinks is between us. But, what if he's doing the only thing he can do to soften up Nigella to get more information? Or, if he has flipped, then he would be forced to stop me. Dead.

When the pipes clank as the shower kicks in, I can't help but smile. Bill's love of a long, hot shower will give me fifteen to twenty minutes—time I need to scope out the rest of the house.

I open each of the next two doors, then try the last of the three on the other side of the hall.

That door is locked. I see that the lock is keyed on this side of the door and press my ear hard against it. Not a sound. It's eight thirty when I exit Walking Rain.

My next move is to alert the law. No matter how inept Senior Deputy Rick Santana is, he has the only access to men and search warrants in Taos County.

CHAPTER 42

I MAKE IT BACK TO MY CABIN, throw my backpack purse on the bed against the pillows, and collapse next to it.

After processing what just happened at Walking Rain, I have come to some conclusions. The Talaveras are very much in league with the Deverings. And Bill?

My feeble hope that he had to set up the relationship with Nigella in order to get inside the drug trafficking scheme died with the sound of her braying.

I grab my cell and dial 411.

"Taos, New Mexico, Sheriff's Department, please," is barely out of my mouth when I feel the press of cold metal against the nape of my neck and hear a soft drawl say, "Hang up, or I'll be forced to use this."

Even though my Beretta is in the backpack purse leaning against my right thigh, there's no way I can get to it without the man getting off the first shot. I raise the cell in his direction. "Okay, okay."

A hand grabs my cell as the weapon leaves the back of my neck.

Tex Bodine settles into the chair across from me and leans forward, Springfield XD—complete with silencer—cradled in the crook of his left arm.

"Sorry about the theatrics, but I couldn't think of any other way to stop you."

"Oh, there are plenty of other ways, but first things first. Do you know where Rebbie is?"

Tex looks down for a few seconds before he says, "That's why I'm here. I was hoping you would know."

I give an involuntary shudder. "Then I take it that means you and Rebbie haven't been in contact?"

He shakes his head. "I haven't seen her since late Thursday night."

I see the anguish in his eyes. He's telling the truth.

At that, another shudder wrenches my gut, accompanied by a sharp wave of panic.

"Did you send Rebbie a note yesterday, asking her to meet you at the Taos Airport?"

"No. Why?"

"Rebbie got a typed note asking her to meet you at Hangar Four at seven last night. I told her it was some sort of setup, and begged her not to go, but she wouldn't listen to me.

"She invited me to her cabin for a five o'clock cocktail so she could tell me good-bye. I went to her cabin at the appointed hour, but the entire place had been sanitized down to a brand-new coverlet on the bed. It was as if Rebbie had never occupied the room at all.

"From there I went to Nigella's office, but she claimed that Rebbie had taken the Navigator to Albuquerque in time to make the afternoon flight."

I start to tell Tex about the locked room in Walking Rain, then realize that, if I do tell him, we'd both be back there as fast as we could make it, and, if it were a false alarm, we would probably be caught.

"I'm really worried. Isn't there anything you can do about this?"

Tex punches a number, listens, then shakes his head and tries a second number. "Her home and cell phones go directly to message. That's not good."

He makes another call. Gives someone on the other end Rebbie's numbers, and then adds that she's his fiancée.

When he snaps his cell shut, I give him the smarmiest smile I can muster. "Gee, thanks for knocking me out, locking me in the shed at the airport, and then leaving me to take the fall for Hernandez's murder."

Tex holds up his hand. "Correction. I wasn't the one who knocked you out, and, just for the record, I didn't kill Hernandez either. What I told both you and Sheriff Hernandez is the truth. I'm FBI, working out of Albuquerque, and I am undercover."

"Is that why you were helping Nigel Devering carry that poor dead girl down the trail?"

"I wasn't on the trail, but I do know who was."

"Care to share?"

"Not at the moment."

"But I heard your voice."

"Did you see me?"

"No. But—"

"My guess is you heard someone who sounds a lot like me. And he does. This man is working with me—on the other side."

"Marva's son?"

That knocks him down a few pegs. "What do you know about that?"

"She told me some people thought you could be twins, though she didn't see much of a resemblance except for your blond hair."

Tex gives a half chuckle. "Actually, Buster and I have been able to pull off a couple of very successful switcheroos. He was the one who helped Santana load Channing into the hearse, while I was snatching her briefcase and changing clothes."

"Then how did you get down the mountain?"

"Let's just say I did." Tex checks his watch then says, "Any more questions? I don't have much time left."

"What about the briefcase?"

"I left it in the sheriff's office. Remember? Then I excused myself to make a call. I was attacked from behind and knocked unconscious. I didn't come to until after eight that night. No briefcase in sight. I'd give my eyeteeth to know where it went."

Tex's answers are a little glib, but he seems to be on the level. We stare at each other for a few seconds before I say, "Marva tells me she's known you for a long time."

He nods. "She helped me get the job at the spa."

"So she said. I went by her house for a visit yesterday. Actually, she was very helpful."

"In what way?"

"She told me the first time she went into the Pilates room, Channing was still alive."

He looks up, eyebrows raised.

"I thought she might have told you that while we were waiting for the sheriff to arrive."

He slowly shakes his head. "No. She never mentioned anything about that to me."

"There was someone else in the house with her yesterday. All of a sudden, she hustled me out the front door, and then took off in her car. Know anything about that?"

He raises his free hand in the air. "Guilty as charged. That was me coming in the back door. Guess Marva didn't want you to see me."

"Do you know why she drove off like a bat out of hell? I'm really worried."

He stares at me for a few seconds, then flips open his phone, punches in a number, and, after a few seconds, nods and grins.

"Marva? It's Tex. You okay?"

She's talking so loudly I can almost hear what she's saying. All the while Tex is nodding.

"That's all I wanted to know. Stay put, ya hear?"

Tex closes the cell. "She did what I asked her to do, only with a little more speed than was necessary. She's got a cabin up at the Ski Valley. She's laying low for a few days until the dust settles. Don't worry. She's fine."

"Why were you at Marva's?"

"I've been using Marva's as a safe house. I can walk to the spa from her house if I have to."

"Really?"

"It's not an easy trek, but very doable. Look, I don't have much time to do what has to be done before the action goes down today. Santana is supposed to have acquired the necessary warrants. He's meeting me at the trailhead with some men at ten thirty."

I raise my hand. "I need to see some proof of just who you are and who you're working for."

"Or you'll what?" He waves his Springfield XD vaguely in my direction.

I shrug. "Nothing, I guess. You're armed; I'm not."

Tex reaches in his back pocket, pulls out his wallet, and lets it flop open to reveal an official-looking badge across from a well-worn identity card. "Does this do the trick?"

I shrug. "Those are a dime a dozen. How do I know it's not a forgery?"

"Actually, you don't. But I don't have time to prove it."

He gives me a thoughtful once-over, then says, "There are a couple of ways to get in and out of this spa undetected, but the best way is"—he pauses—"got a map?"

I pull the trail map from my purse and open it on the bed.

Tex joins me and points to Walking Rain. "The Cibolo Creek Trail is the safest way in and out. Just follow the path from Walking Rain down to the creek and keep going. You'll get off the property after a mile or so. Then the trail becomes part of Carson National Forest.

"It'll take you some time, but it's all downhill, and, eventually, you'll end up in Arroyo Seco."

He holsters his weapon, checks his watch, and says, "Too bad we couldn't get someone into Walking Rain. It would help a lot to know the layout."

At that, I jump in with both feet. "I just came from there. What do you want to know?"

"Everything you can tell me."

I describe, down to the last detail, what I saw in Walking Rain, particularly the bath setups, the long stainless steel table in the kitchen, and the walk-in refrigerator.

I don't mention what was happening in the master suite except to say, "Apparently there's a large suite to the right at the top of the stairs. It was occupied."

Bodine flips open his cell, punches in a number, and repeats what I've just told him.

When he ends the conversation, he reaches out to grab my hand and shake it. "Welcome to the operation. Do you have a weapon? Because if you need one—"

I pull my Beretta 3032 and its holster from my purse. "No problem."

He takes a step back. "That's a surprise. Nobody said you were carrying."

"Nobody asked."

When I start to strap on the holster, he says, "Hold it. Packing heat up here at the spa isn't such a good idea. Just go about your usual routine, but keep your eyes and ears open."

"You're telling me to do nothing?"

"After I leave to meet Santana, you'll be the only one who can give us information from the inside."

Bodine opens my cell, programs two numbers, and hands it back to me. "Don't use these unless you absolutely have to."

He checks his watch. "I'm outta here. Just do the same things you've been doing every day, and you'll be fine."

"What about Rebbie?"

"I won't lie. I'm very worried."

CHAPTER 43

DOING WHAT I "USUALLY DO" for the rest of the day is really hard; knowing what I know now colors every move I make.

At breakfast, I take a seat at my old table for two, wishing that Rebbie were sitting across from me. But, despite a stomach knotted by a mix of fear and excitement, I manage to strangle down some granola with yogurt and fruit, and two cups of Jamaica Blue.

Over the second cup, I take stock of the situation.

Who can I trust?

At this point, Bill is definitely out—Nigella, too—and God knows which of the staff besides the Toles are in the employ of the Talavera cartel.

Bodine is questionable, but he has more checks in the "Good" column than anybody else. If only I'd listened to Rebbie. She knew.

I can't reach Bradford, and the senior deputy is no help at all.

I let out a long, sad sigh, then check the schedule once again. At nine, I have my massage, but it's not with Marva or Helen. Today, I have Glenys. That's followed by a facial at ten, broth at eleven, and then lunch as usual.

The afternoon is wide open, just as it has been since I indicated my preference for hiking, but Bodine warned me away from the trails, saying there's no point in running into someone I might not care to meet, and reminding me there's safety in numbers.

Glenys, today's masseuse, is silent and efficient, and does a deep massage better than any I've ever had.

I slide off the table and into my warm robe, then slink down the hall for my facial.

After a long, hot shower and several cups of warm broth, I return to my cabin, crawl beneath the coverlet, and fall into a dead sleep.

To my amazement, it's well past two when the phone on my bedside table rings.

"Allie, darling? Nigella here. I didn't see you at lunch. Are you all right?"

I quash the bile that rises at the sound of her too, too chirpy voice, along with the initial urge to slam down the phone, then try my best to keep my response as enthusiastic as it would be if I didn't know what went on with Bill only hours before.

"Of course I'm all right. How nice of you to ask. To tell you the truth, I was so relaxed from my massage and facial that I came back here to read until lunch, and fell fast asleep. Actually, I was just going to the kitchen to see if they could fix me a sandwich or something."

"Oh, don't do that. I'll order up some tea and dainties. How does that sound?"

"But—"

"I won't take no for an answer. I haven't had the opportunity to show you my quarters. My suite is in Walking Rain. Do you know where that is?"

I hesitate only a second, now sure that Nigella knows what I was up to early this morning.

"I can only stay a minute. I'm hoping to hike El Prado if the weather keeps. I'll be there as soon as I get dressed."

"Jolly good. See you then."

I drop the receiver into the cradle. Now that I'm fully conscious, I realize what her call means. Trouble.

Bodine had implied that whatever was going to happen would take place after the drug mules arrived at Walking Rain.

But, if everything had gone as planned, Nigella and Bill should be in custody by now.

To hear my new archenemy sounding so chipper sends ice down my spine. It's all too plain that there's been a major glitch in Bodine's plan.

I press the first number he added to my cell and wait for him to answer. When it goes to message, I hang up and try the second. Same response.

The stone in my stomach grows to boulder size.

I unzip the false bottom of my backpack purse and stow both my Beretta and cell there. Then I throw two bottles of water and a couple of granola bars in the upper part of my purse, just in case.

It's then I decide to buy a little insurance by alerting one or more of the staff to where I'll be. With any luck, someone will remember, if I don't turn up for dinner.

I take the path to the main building. Once inside, I stop by registration. When the desk clerk steps forward, I say, "Any messages for Armington? Cabin Four?"

She gives me a pleasant smile and looks toward the empty box. "Sorry."

"Too bad. I'm expecting an important FedEx. Don't they make late afternoon deliveries?"

She consults a card, then checks her watch. "That's right. They usually come between four and five."

"Oh, good. Then there's still a chance I'll get it today. I'm on my way to join Miss Devering for tea at Walking Rain. If my package comes, could you please call me there before you try my cabin?"

After she scribbles a note and sets it by the phone, I exit through the back door and start up Lágrima Del Sol.

CHAPTER 44

NIGELLA GREETS ME at the front door with one of her signa-ture air kisses.

"Welcome to Walking Rain, the star of Cielo Azul's varied offerings to our exclusive clientele. To put it briefly, Walking Rain is our pride and joy."

I ignore the sales pitch. Nigella can save that for those not "in the know."

On the far wall of the living room, a welcoming fire crackles. "Thank heavens the evenings are getting a little nippier. I thought we might have our tea in front of the fireplace, after I show you my suite."

She starts up the stairs without waiting for an answer, and I follow, not exactly sure I want to see where she and Bill had their early morning tryst, but still curious enough to check it out.

The second-floor suite is done in the usual Southwestern motif.

To the left is a cozy sitting area, with French doors opening onto the porch overlooking Cibolo Creek. To the right, across from the sitting area, there's a small dining table in front of a Pullman kitchenette.

Through double doors, a king bed is placed against the wall to the left, across from another set of French doors, these opening onto the porch facing Lower Ranchitos Trail.

On the whole, it's a pleasant area, but one in which I don't want to spend any more time than I have to.

Nigella turns to face me, eyes bright with pleasure. "This is it. I know it's small, but it's really all I need, what with the office in the spa building and the whole downstairs to use when there are no clients."

She seems to be waiting for some sort of reaction, but, when none comes, she glides past me and down the stairs.

After she ushers me into the living room, Nigella points to one of the large leather chairs in front of the fire. "It's so comfy in front of a cozy fire, don't you agree?"

She walks to a nearby table, picks up a telephone receiver, and presses a button.

I hear the phone ringing through the kitchen door. Then Nigella says, "I believe the tea cart should be ready, Irma. Please serve us now. Thank you."

Almost instantly, the whish of a swinging door is followed by the sound of wheels clanking across the uneven Saltillo tiles.

A staff woman I've never seen before struggles with a stubborn tea cart bearing two small silver cover domes, a large silver teapot, and accompanying china.

"Oh dear," I say. "You didn't have to go to all that trouble just for me. As I mentioned when you called, I'm on my way to hike El Prado. I usually don't take any liquid until I start for home base."

Nigella flashes her usual perky smile, and then says, "I don't think a little sip of this will hurt you. It's a special blend of black tea from Tanzania, grown not far from the Ngorongoro Crater. And just wait until you see what I had the kitchen prepare especially for you."

She nods to the woman, who stations the tea cart in front of Nigella's chair, and discreetly disappears.

Nigella removes one of the domes. "Voilá. Cucumber sandwiches, and my absolutely, all-time favorite—pimento cheese. Mother's recipe is outstanding, if I do say so myself."

I've hated pimento cheese since I was a kid and my mother forced a sandwich down me against my will, but there's no point in bringing that up. My goal is to get out of here as fast as I can.

Nigella fills the two cups with tea, and places several of the small sandwiches on each plate.

"Lemon? Sugar? Cream?"

"Nothing, thank you."

She raises her cup. "Allie, dear. I can't begin to tell you how wonderful it is that we've finally reconnected after all these years."

I nod, smile, and take a sip as a delicious aroma curls into my nostrils.

At the second taste, a pleasant tingle tickles my lips. "Mmmm. What did you say this is? It's wonderful."

After I take a third sip, the tingle surfs down both my arms to my fingers. I watch the cup and saucer fall from my hands and separate in slow motion. Drops of tea shimmer and dance in midair, sparkling in the flickering firelight.

The saucer floats to my lap, followed by the now empty cup that continues to drift down to the Navajo rug beneath my feet.

I look up to see Nigella. She's floating, too, in my direction, her feet barely touching the floor.

"Oh, Allie. You've been such a naughty girl." Her voice has a lovely ring to it. I want to hear it again and again.

When I try to speak, no words come, but I really don't care about my words right now; I just want to hear Nigella's.

Bells begin to chime. Beautiful, beautiful, bells.

Nigella wafts to a table, lifts the shimmering telephone receiver to her ear, and sings in the loveliest of voices, "Yes. Come now."

CHAPTER 45

I'M HAVING TROUBLE keeping my eyes open, and I have absolutely no feeling in my body, but I am so wonderfully relaxed. It's obvious that I've been drugged and I don't even give a damn.

It doesn't really matter that I can't feel anything—I'm positive I'll be comfortable wherever I end up. I just know I will.

I hear movement, and force my eyelids open to see a man standing before me.

He's tall and slender. White blond with a mahogany tan. This has to be Nigel Devering because he's the image of his sister. But, what is merely attractive about Nigella, is a knockout on her brother.

His voice, which seems to be coming from an echo chamber, sounds as sibilant as his sister's. "I don't like this one bit, Gella. She has much too high a profile. Too many people know she's here. I hope you and Tole know what you're about."

Nigella's hand floats up to wave his comments away. "Of course we do. But, Nigey, she knows much too much. If Ramón finds out that she breached Walking Rain this morning, and was in here long enough to see everything, I hate to think what he'll do."

Nigel shakes his white blond mane, which rises slowly from his forehead, then resettles. "Don't fret so about Ramón. He trusts us completely. We just have to be careful not to arouse curiosity amongst the other clients."

Nigella's head seems to bob and weave when she responds. "But, Nigey, the doors and windows are double-paned, and the building is completely soundproofed."

"Be that as it may," Nigel says, "I told you right from the beginning that the surveillance system was inadequate. For just a few thousand more, we could have had state-of-the-art in every room."

Nigella's lips seem to slide off her face. "Yes, yes. I know now that it doesn't pay to cut corners."

Nigel looks my way. "Do you realize how much money we lost today because of that nosy bitch? If we hadn't been tipped off this morning, we'd all be cooling our heels in the Taos jail."

"Fortunately, we were able to stop the delivery. We'll be only a little over twenty-four hours behind schedule. The delivery's set for one tomorrow."

Even though I'm having trouble focusing on their conversation, I get the drift. They were tipped off. Was it someone from the sheriff's office? Or was it Bill? But the important thing to remember is the delivery at one tomorrow.

I have to get out of here.

I must have managed to move because, the next thing I know, I'm sliding from the chair to the floor. Nigel rushes over just in time to catch me.

"Damn it, Gella. You gave her too much. She's completely paralyzed. If her involuntary responses fail, she'll die before we can get any information out of her."

"What kind of information do you think she has, Nigey? There's no way on earth she could know anything about Selena."

Nigel smiles. "I must say that was a very slick maneuver—the perfect answer for disposing of that poor, dead, Mexican girl."

With a great deal of effort, he rights me in the chair, then floats out of my sight line. "Need I remind you that, if we lose Allie, we'll have yet another body to get rid of? My God, they're starting to stack up like cordwood."

They? I blink my eyes a couple of times, trying to focus. Who else could there be besides me?

It's then I notice that the aura surrounding Nigella isn't quite as bright as it once was, and that some feeling has returned to my arms.

"I know what I'm doing, Nigey. Tole and I have been working on the proper dosage all week."

I hear the front door open, then footsteps.

When Bill comes into view, Nigella circles his neck with both arms and says, "Darling, what took you so long?"

She turns to someone else and says, "Help Mr. Devering put her on the couch. We'll question her there."

Nigel grabs hold of my ankles as another set of hands slides beneath my armpits. The man at my head tries to lift me, and I can tell Nigel is straining as well.

He says, "She's dead weight. It's the drug. Let's go on 'three,' okay?"

On three, they drag me over the arm of the chair, and then manage to get me the few feet to the couch. Once I'm deposited, the second man comes into view.

"Now what?" he says.

This man isn't Tex Bodine. He's taller and a little heavier, but has the same blond curls and his voice sounds like Tex's.

Marva Weston's voice echoes, *People said they coulda been a pair of twins. But Buster has always outweighed Tex by twenty or thirty pounds.*

He has to be the man who knocked me out—the man who executed the sheriff.

Nigella looms above me with a yellow legal pad in one hand. She rips off a sheet of paper and hands it to Nigel.

"These are the questions. Once she's able to verbalize, we'll have about five minutes."

Nigel shrugs. "I just hope you know what you're doing. One little slip, and it could very easily be over for all of us. Except for Talavera. He's slippery as an eel."

He looks my way, then lowers his voice. "As you recall, the first application of this drug was not at all successful."

CHAPTER 46

THE ROOM IS PITCH-BLACK except for the digital readout from the clock on the bedside table. I squint to read: "4:30."

I yawn, then scrunch into the pillow, hoping to grab a couple of more hours before the early light creeps through the window.

It's a little past six when the daylight does come, and it takes me awhile to work through what seems like a dense fog to become fully aware of my surroundings.

I'm still in the spa warm-up suit, and, after a brief check, realize I've been stashed in one of the upstairs rooms at Walking Rain.

The last clear thing I remember is having tea and sandwiches with Nigella.

There was something strange about the tea. The aroma was wonderfully heady, but my lips began to tingle after I took a taste.

Finally, vague scraps of what happened after I was drugged appear in slideshow fashion, lurching crazily across my mind's eye.

The flashes are often followed by blanks, but, with a lot of effort, I'm able to recall most of the details—the most important being that the drug delivery will be made today at one.

Of course Nigella knew I'd been in Walking Rain that morning. There's a surveillance system. Not state-of-the–art. Nigella had cut corners and Nigel was angry about that.

Why didn't I notice the cameras then? But it wouldn't have mattered if I had seen them. I would have responded to Nigella's invitation anyway.

Wait ... wait. There's something much more important to remember. Then the thoughts I had had such difficulty putting together finally gel.

Selena Channing isn't dead.

Sometime between my last visit to the Pilates room and the departure of the hearse, Selena had managed to slip away, and the Latina's body was placed in the body bag.

I also remember Bill arriving with a man who looked a lot like Tex Bodine. But it wasn't Tex. It was Buster, Marva's son.

By that time, some of the numbness had been wearing off, and, when Nigel and Buster moved me to the couch, I went limp so they would think the drug was still working.

Nigel had questioned me about Bodine and his plans. But I'd mumbled some half-baked answers that seemed to satisfy them.

To my surprise, Bill had volunteered to carry me upstairs. Over Nigella's protests, he'd scooped me into his arms and said to Buster, "Bring along that backpack, okay?"

After Bill had edged me through the door to one of the upstairs rooms, he'd turned to Buster. "Just put the backpack on the floor, pull back that spread, and then you can go."

Once I was settled, Bill's lips had brushed my forehead before he whispered, "Things don't look too promising for you right now, my darling, but, if by some miracle you ever get out of here, and, if you can remember anything about this night, I hope it will be that I loved you."

I'd heard the door close and lock, then waited to cry until his footsteps faded down the hall.

CHAPTER 47

I HAVE TO FACE the fact that whatever Bill and I had is over. And, from the looks of things between Bill and Nigella, it's been over for a very long time.

But, the real tragedy of the situation is that Bill has sacrificed both his personal and professional integrity for a life on the other side of the law.

I check my watch. 6:45. Then I swallow the growing lump in my throat. There's no time for grief now. I have to get out of here.

After studying the layout to orient myself, I realize I'm in a room that faces the front of Walking Rain on Lower Ranchitos Trail.

Bill, ever the neatnik, has placed my hiking boots on the floor next to my backpack purse. After lacing up, I grab my purse and head for the bathroom.

To my relief, I can still feel the outline of my Beretta and cell right where I left them, in the bottom of my purse.

But Bill had to know I was armed. Why didn't he take my weapon? Or my cell? Could it be that he's not such a bad guy after all? Maybe he *is* acting as a double agent.

I push those thoughts aside for now. But, if I ever get away from this spa in one piece, I plan to apologize profusely to my sister. Angela was right about Nigella Devering from the get-go.

I've just stepped back into the bedroom from the bathroom when I hear approaching footsteps.

Clutching my purse to me, I quickly slide beneath the coverlet and turn my back to the door, just as the key slides into the lock.

The door opens.

"I told you she'd still be asleep," Nigella whispers. "With the amount of drugs we gave her she probably won't wake up until midday at the earliest."

But Bill is with her. "What if she doesn't revive by the time the shipment arrives?"

"Not to worry, my love. We'll put her in my suite and deal with her later."

Bill says, "Just the same, I better check to make sure she's still alive."

"What difference does it make, darling? I mean, if she's already dead, it will save later unpleasantness."

I can't let Bill come any closer. He's sure to notice that my boots and purse are missing. I let out a low moan, hoping that will be enough to indicate I'm alive but still in a stupor.

It must work because the door clicks shut, the lock turns, and two sets of footsteps retreat down the hall. After a brief silence, I hear one person clearly descending the stairs, and the front door opens, then shuts.

A few minutes later, the shower comes on.

That gives me a good fifteen minutes to escape—if I'm lucky.

I step onto the porch and look both ways. No one's in sight. Fortunately, there are only a few steps to the stairs that will take me down to the Cibolo Creek side of the house.

I unzip the false bottom of my backpack purse, remove my Beretta, slide it into my jacket pocket, and then check my watch. 7:10.

CHAPTER 48

THE TRAIL FROM Walking Rain to Cibolo Creek, one hundred feet below, takes more time to negotiate than I had imagined. The tortuously steep, extremely narrow path is crisscrossed by root systems, making each downward step an arduous effort.

Worse still, the mist rising from the rushing creek has added to the difficult descent by creating a very slippery slope.

It's almost 7:35 by the time I reach the water's edge, and, remembering Tex's instructions, follow the downward path, keeping the creek to my right.

I shove my right hand into my jacket pocket and grip my Beretta. There's a bullet in the chamber and the safety is off—not a good idea when the path is this treacherous, but absolutely necessary in case I run into trouble.

After twenty minutes or so, the pitch of both creek and path begins to even out. The canyon walls rise steeply on both sides of the creek, allowing the stands of tall spruce and fir to merge and obstruct a clear view of the sky.

Then the path widens. A sign facing the trail with an arrow pointing to where I've just been reads: "Private Property of SpaCo, Ltd. No Trespassing. All Trespassers Will Be Prosecuted."

It's such a relief to be off spa lands, I almost feel like I'm home free.

The path ahead is fairly smooth, allowing me to pick up the pace. I judge that I've covered about two miles when I spot a large rock. A sign reads: "Mesa Rock Rest Area. No Facilities Available." It's the perfect place to stop for a few minutes, munch on a power bar, and swig some water.

I settle on the rock and study the area. Lots of footprints. A couple of cigarette butts. An empty matchbook.

A glint near the creek catches my attention. It's an expended shell casing. After a thorough search, I find one more. I check my watch. 8:50.

I put the casings in my backpack and head on down the trail.

I stop again, this time to try my cell. No signal.

After another forty minutes, I arrive at a parking area marked by a sign for the Carson National Forest Cibolo Creek Trailhead. There are only a few cars, but that doesn't surprise me since it's a workday.

I plod ahead out of the parking area and on to El Salto Road.

A fifteen-minute walk brings me to Seco Plaza, a picturesque little shopping area in Arroyo Seco. I settle on one of the benches, check to see that it's almost 9:45, and try my cell.

After getting the number from Information, I'm connected to Senior Deputy Santana's office.

CHAPTER 49

SANTANA LETS OUT a groan when I tell him who it is. "It can't be you. You're supposed to be long gone by now. Don't you know how to quit when you're ahead of the game?"

"Sorry to disappoint you, but I've come across some very important information concerning your uncle's murder. Is it possible for you and several of your men to meet me at Seco Plaza in Arroyo Seco?"

"Arroyo Seco?" It's hard to overlook the exasperation in his voice. "Give me one good reason why I should rush out to Arroyo Seco with my men just because you ask me to?"

"Look, I wouldn't be calling if this weren't urgent. We don't have much time."

"Take the time to convince me, okay?"

I check my watch. I've been on my cell several minutes already. What can I say to jump-start this yahoo?

"What happened to the raid you were supposed to make yesterday? Bodine told me you and your men were going to be stationed on Cibolo Creek below Walking Rain."

"You saw Tex? When?"

When I hear the surprise and urgency in Santana's voice, a creepy feeling—accompanied by that stone in my stomach—comes over me.

"Early yesterday morning. He was on his way to meet you."

"He never showed," Santana says. "We waited for him in the trailhead parking area for two hours. That means they must have caught him."

"That's what I was afraid of. And, if that's so, then I'm pretty sure someone from your office told the Deverings to call off the drug delivery yesterday."

"What did you say?"

"Someone had to alert the Deverings. I don't think it was Bodine. So it has to be someone who was in on the raid."

"I'm positive no one knew in the office. Besides, I trust these men. They were my uncle's compadres. They've looked after me since I came to live with him."

"I'm not going to waste time arguing with you. If you trust your men, then fine. But, since it looks like Bodine's out of the picture for now, you're going to have to make a judgment call. They're planning to make the delivery today at one o'clock. You don't have much time if you want to end up the big hero in town."

I have to admit Santana used remarkable restraint as well as speed. It's just past 10:20 when two unmarked cars pull to the curb in front of the bench where I sit, and the senior deputy walks over to settle beside me.

I reach in my backpack and search the bottom for the shell casings. "I found these at Mesa Rock. But I didn't see any blood or signs of a scuffle."

Santana takes one casing and checks it out. "Could be from any standard issue automatic."

He slumps back against the bench and lets out a long breath. "So that must be what happened. Somebody caught up with Bodine before he could get to us."

I sadly nod my agreement. "All I know is the shipment is definitely scheduled for today. Do you still have the necessary search warrants?"

He pats his jacket pocket. "Right here."

"That's good. Without them any arrests or confiscations won't mean a thing."

"Damn! I don't think we can do this without Bodine."

"You have to. This may be your only chance. If the cartel does have Bodine, they know the feds are onto them, and they won't bring the drugs in this way again."

I hesitate only a few seconds before adding, "Look, I can lead you in. As I said, the van isn't supposed to arrive at Walking Rain until one. That's well over two hours from now."

I glance over at the two unmarked cars. There are four men in one and three in the other. If Santana agrees to let me lead, I'll make nine.

I go over the possible players in Walking Rain: the Deverings, the Toles, Bill, Buster, Weston, and possibly six men who do the cutting and packaging.

"There are, at the minimum, four men and two women in Walking Rain that I know of. One is a doctor—not that that means anything these days. One of the women is a nurse. But what I don't know is exactly how many men are cutting and packaging."

Santana shakes his head. "If we do this right now, I won't have time to call in any more men."

"I understand. There were six stools at the processing center located in the kitchen. That would make twelve bad guys at the most. There are only nine of us, but I think we have the advantage in surprise and weaponry.

"And we have to get these people today. I know the layout of Walking Rain, and how to get where we need to go without revealing ourselves."

"Even so …"

"There's also something else you should know. I'm positive the man who killed your uncle is at Walking Rain right now. Wouldn't you like to be the one to bring him in?"

"You bet I would. Getting his murderer won't bring Uncle Oscar back, but it would sure make all of us who loved him feel a lot better."

Santana stands. "How long will it take?"

"From the trailhead, it's probably two hours plus, max, if we keep up the pace."

Santana shakes his head. "That's a long time. Why not drive it?"

"Right. And let's be sure to use the sirens. Then the guard can stall us at the gatehouse until the Deverings have time to get rid of the evidence, disperse the mules, and go on about business as usual."

I grab his arm. "Don't you get it? The element of surprise is our only advantage—provided that the man who ratted you out yesterday isn't in one of those two cars."

I pause, then say, "If he is, it already may be too late. He may have contacted the Deverings the minute he saw me."

Santana looks toward the cars. "He'd have had to get out of the car to make the call, or the others would have heard him and figured it out."

I stand and check my watch. "It's just past ten thirty. We should be able to catch these people, if we get going now."

CHAPTER 50

TO MY SURPRISE, the return to Walking Rain seems to go more quickly and easily than my escape had.

The only time Santana asks us to take it slowly is between the trailhead and Mesa Rock. Half of us are to check the thick undergrowth to the right, and half to comb the edges along the creek to the left, for some evidence of what might have happened to Tex Bodine.

Luckily, no one sees any blood or results of a struggle. Maybe Bodine made it to some sort of safe haven after all. But, if that were true, wouldn't he have contacted Santana by now?

It's a little past 12:45 when we begin our rise from Cibolo Creek to Walking Rain—almost a cakewalk compared to my descent. The roots that were so treacherous then, now serve as aids in the upward climb.

Once we are above the rising mist, I stop. The next few minutes will be the trickiest to maneuver.

I motion Santana to join me, and we climb to a spot just below the top of the trail. From there we can see the building, but are still safe from being spotted from the second-floor porch.

"As you can see, Walking Rain is a long, narrow, two-story building with deep porches upstairs and downstairs. Those porches should give us an advantage since the French doors that open onto them make it difficult to see what's going on outside.

"Downstairs is a living room, dining room, and a kitchen. Upstairs above the living room are six small bedrooms with baths— three on either side of a central hallway. Miss Devering's suite is at the far end above the kitchen.

"The drugs are unloaded in the bathrooms upstairs. It's a very efficient setup. Two mules share a bath. At a time dictated by the whims of their digestive tracts, the pellets are excreted, hosed down, and placed in plastic bags.

"As best I can guess, the pellets are then counted and weighed in the kitchen. Then the drugs are cut and processed for distribution.

"After they have 'delivered' their consignments, the women are given $5,000 each, driven back to the airport, and flown back to Baja. In short, the operation is a slick, well-oiled, billion-dollar bonanza for the Talavera cartel."

Santana clears his throat a couple of times, but still squeaks when he asks, "Did you say Talavera? That cartel operates on the Pacific coast, doesn't it?"

I shake my head. "There was a turf war several years ago. They moved their operations to Mexicali."

Santana gives me a questioning look. "And you're sure the Talaveras are involved?"

"I'd lay my life on it."

He takes a deep breath, squares his shoulders, then checks his weapon and flips off the safety. "Well, I guess I'm as ready as I'll ever be. What do we do next?"

My mouth drops. "Don't you know?"

He shrugs.

I look into that earnest, expectant face, and let out a long sigh. What irony. I've brought Santana and his men to this point, only to discover that there is no plan.

"Didn't Bodine give you some idea of what you and your men were to do once you got here?"

Santana slowly shakes his head. "Bodine just told me to get the necessary warrants and bring my men to the trailhead parking area. He said he would take it from there."

I look behind and down to see the seven others of our "assault" team, and my heart folds. "Ever accompanied your uncle on a raid?"

"No." He slowly shakes his head. "Uncle Oscar didn't take me on any raids."

"Has any of your men ever been on a raid?"

"What would we raid? We mainly cover incidents like burglaries, domestic violence, assaults. Usually drunks who get into bar fights, and stuff like that. There have been some incidents involving drugs, but, if what Bodine told me is true, we've never seen anything near this big."

Boy, is he right about that. But we're here, and we are the only barrier between the Talavera cartel and their bonanza. If we can subdue the people inside Walking Rain and take those drugs, Santana will be a hero.

"Okay then. Our main mission will be to capture as many as we can of the men in the kitchen, cutting the drugs.

"The medical team should be upstairs, monitoring the progress of the drug deliveries.

"Since there are no windows on the fireplace side facing us, I think our best chance would be to gather on the other side of the building—one man at a time.

"You go first. Once you make it and get the lay of the land, you signal me. I'll send the others in, one by one, and then bring up the rear.

"If by some miracle we make it that far, we'll then have to figure how to enter the building without being discovered. If they do catch us, it'll have to be every man for himself."

Santana nods and begins to make his way back down the path to talk to his men.

When he gets halfway to the creek bed, I turn back to continue my surveillance of the house. Minutes pass. No activity.

I'm just turning away to check Santana's progress when Bill and Nigella step out of her living room onto the upstairs porch.

From the looks of it, the two have been arguing. Nigella's waving her arms and Bill's mouth is clamped in that determined straight line I've come to know so well.

I duck, release the safety on my Beretta, and peer through the undergrowth just in time to see Bill raise a major pair of binoculars.

After making a couple of sweeps in my direction, he lowers them, shakes his head, then checks his watch and shakes his head again.

Nigella puts both arms around Bill's neck and murmurs something; the straight line curves into a smile.

I watch as my ex-fiancé plants a lengthy kiss on Nigella's upturned mouth, and then, arm in arm, the two go inside.

I brush aside a sudden rush of jealousy, and force myself to concentrate on what might happen in the next few minutes.

It's then the startling truth comes with such clarity that it almost knocks me from my perch.

Of course Nigella and Bill know I'm gone. They intended for me to escape, but just not quite as early as I did. That's the only reason Bill let me get away armed and able to call for help.

The stone in my gut grows yet again as I realize what a patsy I've been. Bill is banking on the fact that my insatiable curiosity and unquenchable desire to be in the middle of the action will result in my bringing Santana and his men back with me. It's plain as day. We've been set up, and it's my fault.

It's a little after one. The good news is Bill and Nigella don't know exactly what time I left Walking Rain, nor how long it took me to make it to Arroyo Seco. They can only guess.

And, from the expression on Bill's face after he looked at his watch, it doesn't seem like he expects anything to happen right away.

I let out a sigh of relief. If we move in the next few minutes, we'll still have the element of surprise.

CHAPTER 51

IT TAKES TWENTY MINUTES to get the eight men across the back lawn to the front porch of Walking Rain.

I'm just about to make my trip when Nigella appears alone on the upstairs porch. From the state of her clothing, it looks like she and Bill have been indulging in some pretty torrid midday activities.

She brings the binoculars to her eyes, makes a couple of cursory sweeps, then disappears through the door to her living area.

Just as Santana peers around the far corner of the building to motion me on, a hand grabs my right ankle.

Praying that my attacker isn't armed, I raise my left foot, hoping to hurt him enough so he'll loosen his hold.

Before I can execute the action, a familiar voice says, "It's me. Tex."

The adrenaline rush fades as quickly as it came, leaving me limp with relief.

When Tex climbs next to me, the only way I can get my guts back in place is to punch his shoulder with my fist. "Where in hell have you been?"

"Thank God I made it before you started in there."

"I know. It's a setup."

He smiles. "Smart lady. I knew you had brains."

"But where have you been?"

"I was on my way to meet Santana when I ran into Buster down at Mesa Rock. He told me the delivery was called off until today because of the rat in Santana's nest."

"Buster told you? But he was the one who knocked me senseless and killed the sheriff."

Tex shakes his head. "You're dead wrong on that score, Allie. As I told you yesterday, Buster works for me."

"But, if it wasn't Buster, then who was it?"

Tex looks down, then says, "Who do you think?"

"Bill?"

Why is that the first name out of my mouth? And why is Bill the only one who comes to mind?

"Don't you get it? He was after Channing's briefcase, but I beat him to it. My best guess is that Cotton must have overheard you, me, and the sheriff talking in the hall, and, when I stayed behind, he coldcocked me."

Tears push at the back of my eyes, but I force them away. Bill's already betrayed me with Nigella, so what's new?

Tex breaks in. "Okay, back to business. I got here as fast as I could. As far as I can tell from the activity up there, it's business as usual."

"Please tell me you have a plan. I've had to run this exercise off the top of my head since Santana doesn't know diddly."

"So far you've done exactly what I had in mind. How did you figure out that an upstairs entry would be disastrous?"

"I was up there, remember? There's no way out except the main stairs. But what do we do once we all get to the front porch?"

"First, there is no 'we.' I have no intention of putting you in the line of fire."

"That's real gentlemanly of you, but they have at least twelve people on their side. Now that you're here, the two of us will make it an almost equal lineup."

Tex must figure that arguing with me is a waste of time because he pushes upward and motions me along.

As we begin to move, he says, "Okay. Here's the plan. The way I see it, our best approach is to use the front door."

"But what if it's locked? It's a pretty sturdy door. You'll make a lot of noise kicking it in."

"We all have silencers. I can shoot out the lock."

I reach in my jacket pocket and check to be sure my safety is back on. Since I don't have a silencer, I don't want my weapon accidentally to discharge when I cross to the house.

Tex says, "I'll go first, brief the men, then you come when I signal to you. Okay?"

I watch him make his way across the yard, then disappear around the corner of the house.

CHAPTER 52

AFTER WAITING, crouched and ready to make my dash, for well over ten minutes, it finally dawns that Tex never had any intention of including me in the raid.

That makes me angry enough to extract some form of revenge the next time I see him, but I'm not stupid. Whatever is going on inside is hopefully proceeding well enough without me.

I ease off my haunches to settle behind the hedge surrounding Walking Rain, leaning against the post that marks the beginning of the downward trail to Cibolo Creek. Even from that relaxed position, I would be able to spring into action with a few added seconds.

After another ten minutes pass I'm about to holster my weapon when I hear footsteps on the upstairs porch.

I peer through bushes to see Bill and Nigella at the top of the stairs that lead down to the ground. Bill has his weapon clutched in his right hand, his left holds onto Nigella's right hand.

A door slams and Bill pushes her away to take a few steps down the stairs, then motions for her to join him.

He says something to Nigella and she moves behind him and circles his waist.

When Bill raises his left hand to steady his aim, I don't even think twice. I slide the safety off and train my Beretta in their direction as I rise from behind the hedge, go through the open gate, and make my way toward them.

Lucky for me neither sees me because their attention is focused on the top of the stairs.

By the time Bill realizes that no one is following him I've reached the bottom of the stairs and taken my stance.

Nigella peers around Bill. "Oh, my God, it's Allie."

Bill turns my way and trains his weapon on me. "Put that down, Allie. There are two of us and only one of you."

I smile. "I believe that's to your disadvantage, not mine."

He smiles back. It's that quirky endearing smile I first fell for in Uvalde. "But, you only have time to get off one shot. Think—"

His voice fades. I'm at the shooting range outside Lampasas. My father's words replay: *It's a gentle action, Allie. The motion should be more like a sigh than a gasp. It's vital that you squeeze the trigger as if it were a delicate flower. Gentle action will assure that your aim won't falter. Squeeze too hard and you'll lose the target.*

I see a strange look cross Bill's face, but before he can utter a word, I squeeze.

The impact of the bullet slamming into his body pitches him backwards and Nigella, arms still clasped around his waist, goes down with him.

Nigella rolls toward Bill. "Darling?" She pats frantically at his shoulder. "Darling? Open your eyes, please. . .open your eyes."

I hear footsteps on the upstairs porch and then Tex, weapon at the ready, appears.

He descends several steps to where Bill and Nigella are lying, feels for Bill's carotid, then looks at me and slowly shakes his head.

Nigella stares up at Tex for a few seconds. Then the realization of what he means hits her.

She whirls to face me and screams, "You bitch. You. . .murderer!"

I watch numbly as she struggles to her feet, then rushes down the stairs, sobbing uncontrollably.

I know I should try to defend myself. But all I can hear is Nigella's accusation running through my brain.

I want to shout, "But Bill was armed. He aimed his gun at me."

Too late. Nigella clutches my neck with both her hands pressing her thumbs into my windpipe as she screams "murderer" again and again.

CHAPTER 53

CONFUSION REIGNS FOR THE NEXT FEW MINUTES as Santana's deputies swarm out of the house with weapons aimed at the backs of the drug traffickers.

I'm seated on the ground. Head between my legs hoping the black spots dancing in my eyes will disappear.

Tex is holding a struggling Nigella several feet away from me until one of Santana's men returns to cuff her.

As she passes by us, she turns my way to glare, and then spit in my direction as she mouths "Murderer" one last time. Then the deputy guides her out of sight.

Several minutes pass before the EMTs arrive, park the gurney, and climb the steps. They kneel next to Bill and slowly unfold a body bag. There's the offending zip of the zippers, then the EMTs awkwardly descend to hoist the body bag on the gurney, buckle the straps, and disappear around the corner.

For some reason I feel nothing. It's like I'm watching a play. Soon the curtain will come down and raise again to reveal Bill and Nigella smiling while taking their bows.

Won't it?

Bodine picks up my weapon and hands it to me. "Just want to give you a head's up. When we talk to the Sheriff, we might have a little trouble explaining what just happened."

"Trouble? What just happened? What do you mean?"

He shrugs and steers me along the path toward my cabin. "Well, I guess you could say you shot first because you thought he was armed. . .although. . ."

Why am I suddenly shivering? I saw Bill steady himself to fire. I heard him say I would only have a chance to get in one shot.

I grab Tex's arm and pull him to a halt. "Are you saying Bill wasn't armed? Because, if that's what you're saying, you're dead wrong. Bill was going to kill me. I wouldn't have shot if I didn't know that for a fact."

"But, Allie, even though I didn't have time to make a real thorough search, I didn't find a gun, the gun you say you saw."

"That can't be. Ask Nigella."

Tex nods. "Let's go get your stuff. Santana wants us down in Taos as soon as we can make it. And once we wrap things up with him, we can ask Nigella about the weapon then."

I give him a wordless nod. "I need a shower."

"Okay. I have some things I need to follow up on, so I'll be back for you in about an hour."

I want to ask him about Rebbie but the words won't form. I'm too afraid to know the truth.

When I exit the bathroom, Tex is there. He tries to smile, and fails. "I just checked with Santana. It's over. They got them all—even the poor women from Mexico. Those sad little ladies, they're scared to death. I don't know what they're going to do with them. Put 'em in jail too, I guess."

I finally feel strong enough to take the blow I know is coming, but my words come out in a hoarse croak. "And Rebbie?"

Tex shakes his head. I see his eyes mist before he quickly turns away to hide his tears.

His words strain through his anguish. "She didn't make it. Those bastards OD'd her then stashed her body in the walk-in refrigerator."

When his shoulders heave, I take the couple of steps separating us to put my arms around him, wanting to somehow say the magic words that will give him needed comfort.

Instead all that comes is an inadequate, pathetic, "I'm so sorry. So sorry."

After offering condolences on Rebbie's untimely death, antana picks up a file and opens it. "Thanks for sharing your information with me, Tex. You've compiled quite a case against Cotton and the Deverings."

I turn to look at my new ally. "You've been keeping a file on Bill?"

He nods. "Remember when I told you and Sheriff Hernandez that I was working with the DEA on a related project? Well, that project was Bill Cotton."

Santana hands a second file to Tex. "I'm returning this. Hope you don't mind that I made copies."

"No, not at all. I'm just anxious to hear what you've found out about the Deverings."

"It didn't take long for them to spill their guts. Of course they realize they're in deep doo-doo and are hoping that if they rat out everybody else connected with the operation, the Feds will go easy. Fat chance of that."

Tex holds up his hand. "Hate to bust your bubble but deals are made all the time. In fact, the Feds can be quite generous to cooperating witnesses—on occasion."

Santana looks up. "You've got to be kidding."

"Wish I was, good buddy, but it's true."

He stares at Tex for a minute and shakes his head. "I know you two want to get out of here as quick as possible, but you might be real interested in what the Deverings offered up."

He turns to me. "Especially you, Miss Armington, since it seems your planned trip to the spa was what set things in motion."

"What do you mean by that?"

"Miss Devering and Agent Cotton have been lovers since early June. In fact they've been inseparable."

Tex frowns and shakes his head. "Let's move on, okay? Miss Armington doesn't have to hear any of this. What's the point? Cotton is dead."

CHAPTER 54

THE TRIP DOWN THE SWITCHBACK and along the
to Taos is made in silence since both Tex and I are lo
own separate hells.

I don't remember passing the lovely Pueblo-style arc
in the center of Taos, or turning into the parking lot of
County Courthouse, but before we mount the stairs to th
floor, Tex says, "Look, Allie, it's entirely possible the iss
whether Bill had a weapon might not come up. After all
bad guy and, as we know, all bad guys carry guns."

"That's ridiculous. I shot and killed a man. And if he di
a gun, then I'm a murderer. But he had a gun, aimed right

Tex raises his hand. "Okay, okay. I believe you, b
doesn't come up then don't bring it up. Okay? Santana's n
to want to initiate an investigation unless he's forced into

Tex finally gets me to promise that I'll keep quiet,
climb the stairs.

Once we're seated across the desk from Senior Deputy
I'm stunned to see the obvious changes in him. Thoug
aware of his metamorphosis from a grief-stricken bumb
to a sadder but aging young man, I now detect a newly
confidence and control. In my opinion, Rick Santana ju
turn into a mighty fine sheriff some day.

Bill is dead.

Bill is dead.

Bill is dead.

Suddenly it's not words anymore.

Bill is dead.

I push the tears to the back of my eyes. "Please. I need to hear everything. Go on."

The senior deputy looks at Tex. "It's your case. You want to tell her?"

"No. Not really. You go ahead. It helps to go through a file verbally. You can retain a lot more information that way. And you'll need to remember the facts when you testify."

The deputy nods, flips the page, and reads a few lines. "Cotton was asked to resign his DEA post last April. No reason given. But from what it says here, the feds were suspicious of his connections to a Colombian drug family as well as his having a longtime association with the Talaveras."

He looks up at Tex, "Anything more on that?"

"I asked a few of the guys who worked with Cotton about what went down, and, for the most part, I got stiffed. But one of them told me Cotton was lucky he didn't have to serve time."

Santana flips a couple of pages. "Says here after Cotton left the DEA he was kept under twenty-four-seven surveillance. By you, Tex?"

Tex nods. "He stayed in Mexicali with the Talaveras for most of April and May."

I start at that, remembering how Bill had told me he was at Quantico separating from the DEA. I never questioned him about what he was doing. All his calls came from the same cell number. Bill could have been in darkest Africa for all I knew, but, at the time, I guess I didn't care about what I knew.

In June his calls had staggered to a halt. When I asked why, Bill explained saying he was sent to the Lesser Antilles on covert assignment.

Santana breaks through my thoughts. "Hey, Bodine, says here you followed Cotton to Baja. How was the spa?"

"I never got there. Cotton was scheduled to visit Cielo Azul next so I hightailed it up here and contacted Marva. By the time Cotton arrived a few days later, I was hired and in place.

"Nigella was delighted to have me on board. Seems staff turnover is pretty common at Cielo because the spa is so remote."

I swivel to face him. "You've known about this all along? Why didn't you say something?"

Tex shrugs. "I couldn't blow my cover. Believe you me, Nigella and Cotton weren't the only ones who were surprised when your sister booked a reservation for the two of you last August. Until that time you were an unknown.

"Thank God I was able to plant a few bugs in Nigella's office and in her suite at Walking Rain.

"Their conversations were pretty revealing. If I hadn't over-heard them talking about you arriving at the same time they were starting up the drug operation from Baja to Taos, you would have been just another name on a reservation card."

It's then I realize, I would probably never have heard from Bill again if it hadn't been for Angela's impetuous decision to book us into that exclusive spa she was reading about in *Travel & Leisure* magazine.

"The next morning Ramón and Nigel arrived. The four of them were holed up in Walking Rain for most of the day.

"They decided there was only one way to stop you and your sister: send Bill to Houston to try and head you off.

So there it finally was. At the Talaveras' "request," Bill had bitten the bullet and resurfaced to stand at my front door with an eager, expectant look on his face, telling me he was done with the DEA and how anxious he was to start our new life together.

And, then when Bill failed in his mission to sidetrack me, Talavera sent his cousin Selena Channing to divert attention from the trafficking operation by "playing dead." There was just one thing they overlooked. The Talaveras hadn't counted on my new found passion—hiking.

The tiny discrepancies, once so easy to overlook, now loom like major red flags. Why didn't I see them then? Was I too much in love with the false image I created? Was I too blind to see it was all a charade? Am I doomed to make the same pathetic mistakes with every man I love?

Those are rhetorical questions.

Are there rhetorical answers, too?

CHAPTER 55

IT'S RAINING. Of course it's raining. It's Houston. The thump, thump, thump of the windshield wipers and Angela's chirpy patter about D3's latest antics only make my head hurt worse.

I've had this headache ever since—how long has Bill been dead?

Or maybe it started when Nigella called me a murderer and then practically strangled the life out of me.

All I know is the dull persistent ache is in protest to my clenched teeth and tensed neck muscles. Let's face it. Every thought I've had since I killed Bill has been weighted with guilt accompanied by bottomless sorrow.

And those are the high points.

Tex and I got through the meeting with Santana without anybody mentioning Bill's "missing" weapon, but by the time we finally signed off on everything, it was really too late to drive to Albuquerque.

When he proposed we take a couple of rooms at El Monte Segrado and start out fresh the next day, I happily agreed. What I needed most was a decent night's sleep.

After we registered, Tex steered me toward the Anaconda Bar, saying that a nice martini was the answer to all our problems.

But downing two martinis only ratcheted up the dull ache to an insistent throb.

Why do we need skulls when all they do is make dumb decisions and then hurt real bad?

Why do we need hearts when. . . ditto.

When a woman suddenly materialized and introduced herself as one of Tex's old friends, I knew I had the perfect out.

He barely nodded when I made my excuses, so I left them, went to my room, and crashed.

Needless to say, this morning I felt anything but fresh. Even the thirty-minute steaming shower did zilch. Finally, the throb sent me to the hotel sundries counter where I purchased a bottle of liquid gel caps.

No victory there. Taking the meds didn't achieve even a pyrrhic beachhead against the cannons pounding at the back of my brain.

Once the plane was in the air, two Bloody Marys, or was it three, finally pitched me into a semi-coma that lasted until I landed, and, through my pounding haze, found Angela impatiently waiting in the baggage area.

And now, here we are in front of my building.

When Eldon the doorman opens the passenger door, I mumble my thanks, grab my stuff out of the back seat, and lurch past him into the empty lobby.

The phone pulls me out of my stupor and Angela whines, "You didn't even say goodbye. What's wrong?"

"Nothing. Not one thing. I'm just exhausted and my head aches—that's all."

"How can you be exhausted and have a headache, you've just come back from a spa?"

I grit my teeth. That makes the headache worse. Still, I can't blame my sister. I haven't told her anything about what happened after Duncan whisked her back to the safety of their McMansion in River Oaks.

And why should I spill my guts? Why should I tell her what a stupid fool I've been? What a heinous thing I did?

I hide my sad sigh and try perky. "You're right about that. Guess I'm just a little down."

"Down? You? Not Miss I'm-so-in-control!" She hurries on. "Remember the pain pills the doc gave me for my C-section? They'd be the perfect remedy for your headache, and, if I recall, there are quite a few left. Bad news is, no refill without calling the doctor. You know how picky they are about giving out too many pills at once."

Angela's voice fades as I remember how woozy she was that first couple of days after she came home with D3. She couldn't hold his bottle long enough to feed him. Sounds like just what I need. "Oh, Angela, if you could. . .that would be wonderful."

"Great. I'm just on my way to Central Market. I'll grab the bottle and drop it off."

Eldon calls first and then brings me the pills swathed in lime green tissue inside a hot pink paper sack.

"Your sister said you needed this pronto."

This time the smile I give him is genuine. Relief is only minutes away.

When I come to, it's dark. I roll to check the time on my digital clock but the numbers squiggle and jump until I squint to make out that it's a little past five.

The aching throb that the two pills diminished to just-above-dull is back with a vengeance. I want to scream because just maybe if I scream, the pain will go away.

Instead I snap on the bedside lamp, take two more pills, and, once the room goes dark again, I lie back.

The trouble is I can't stop Nigella's voice from repeating "murderer" over and over again. And I can't stop seeing Bill lurch back at the impact of my shot.

I roll to my side and let the tears leak into the pillow until I finally fall asleep.

Still dark. Still in pain. Two more pills should do it. Two more pills should make me forget about killing Bill. I'm so close to putting this behind me. Two more pills. Just two more.

I grope through the darkness to find the bottle. The cap is off. The bottle is empty. It can't be empty. I couldn't have taken them all. Could I? Maybe I knocked the bottle over and the pills are on the floor.

I find the light switch, cringe at the searchlight glare, and scan the rug. No pills.

I squint at the label. Two pills then one every four hours not to exceed—

Oh, my God.

My heart lurches into a thready tattoo as my throat constricts in panic. It takes all the strength I have left to punch 911.

CHAPTER 56

I COME OUT OF THE FOG to see Angela sitting next to the bed but it's not my bed. Not my room. The walls behind her are that dreadful institutional green.

Angela gives me a tremulous smile, then leans forward and slips her hand in mine. "Awake at last."

I manage to mutter, "Where am I?"

"This is Doctor Solomon's clinic. We brought you here last night after—"

She raises her eyes to look at someone standing to my right.

Dr. David Solomon, the psychiatrist who helped me to regain my memory several years before, after another trauma, steps into view, to give me a concerned smile.

He opens his mouth to speak but Angela breaks in, eyes filled, and hands wringing. "I'm so sorry, Allie. It's all my fault. I realized something was wrong when I met the plane, but by the time I dropped you at the condo, you seemed pretty much your usual self."

Angela dabs her tears with a soggy ball of Kleenex. "I never should have sent you those pills. What on earth was I thinking? If you hadn't called nine-one-one. . ."

Did I call 911? I must have. But I don't want to think about that right now. Thinking about what happened hurts.

I close my eyes and turn away from her but the assault continues. "When the EMTs arrived, Eldon called us and Duncan and I got there just as they were loading you into the ambulance."

Why can't she just go away? Stop talking. Let me sleep.

"Thank God for Duncan. He knew one of the EMTs and talked him into letting me ride in the back with you since they were taking you to a private clinic."

When she pauses to grab another Kleenex and blow her nose a couple of times, her earlier words finally compute.

I open my eyes and raise up on my elbows. "You think I was planning to—? No! Not suicide. I wouldn't."

Solomon takes the chair next to me. "Under normal circumstances, I would agree, Allie. But you've been under a great deal of stress since. . ." He pats my hand and gives me an encouraging smile.

I shake my head. "I'm telling you, I didn't take those pills to kill myself. It was the damn headache. I just wanted the pounding to stop."

I turn toward Angela to block out his solicitous concern. "Mother and Dad? You haven't told—"

"Don't you remember? They're in Wilmette visiting the Other Armingtons. And when they do call it's all about D3."

At the sound of my nephew's name I realize that any hope for a child of my own with Bill has ended. I ended it when I killed him.

At that, unbidden sobs push forth.

"What's wrong?" Angela looks toward Dr. Solomon. "Did I say something I shouldn't have?"

Two weeks have passed since I almost "adiosed." Dr. Solomon is now seeing me as an out-patient, though it took me several days to convince the man that despite my guilt-laden depression, I have absolutely no intention of ever offing myself. No intention of doing it intentionally. And no intention of doing it unintentionally, either, I think. I mean, I'm sure.

We're just passing the halfway mark in our latest session when he leans forward to take my hand. His voice is soft and soothing. "But, Allie, you shot in defense. That isn't murder."

I rapidly shake my head as tears come. "But I killed the man I was planning to spend the rest of my life with."

Solomon sighs. "I think you're a little confused about exactly what happened at the spa."

My answer is thick with sarcasm. "Oh, yes, I forgot. You were in Taos and saw the whole thing. Don't feed me that bunch of crap. I know exactly what happened."

Solomon gives me his patented gentle-smile. "Then you're saying you shot Bill because he was cheating on you? Not because he was involved in the trafficking of drugs?"

"What difference does it make? He's dead. Please, I don't want to talk about this any more."

"But, isn't it true that you were trying to stop him from escaping?"

"I don't know." I wail. "Don't you think I want to remember what happened?"

Solomon's voice weaves through my protests.

"And, as I've said to you many times before, remembering is the key, Allie. Until you can remember exactly what happened and what you were thinking, you can't go forward."

Solomon pauses, waiting for me to say something but I don't have anything else to say.

I shut my eyes—anything to block his penetrating stare.

Solomon pats my hand. "Look at me, Allie. You have to concentrate on what I'm about to say."

He pauses then says very slowly and carefully, "According to the Senior Deputy Sheriff of Taos County, New Mexico, you acted in the line of duty. In fact Deputy Santana said that if it hadn't been for you, the two might have escaped."

"No, no, no. That's all wrong. Don't you see? It doesn't matter what 'they' think or what 'they' say. I'm a murderer. Nigella Devering said I was. And she was the only other one there."

CHAPTER 57

THANKSGIVING

I PEER INTO THE ORNATE MIRROR perched above the powder room sink to see a pathetic rendition of Allie Armington staring back.

Hair okay. Just not as lustrous as it once was. Lipstick okay. Color in my cheeks? Zip, zero, nada.

I open my purse, find a makeup brush and add a touch of blush to perk up my sallow skin. Then I do a quick reappraisal. Actually, on the surface, and despite the rheumy eyes, I look fairly passable.

It's the stone in my stomach that refuses to go away. My gut knows what I did.

Besides the anti-depressant he has prescribed, Dr. Solomon has practically done handstands to pull me out of my despair, but despite the fact that the meds have kicked in and my crying jags are less frequent, I haven't changed the verdict I handed down on myself.

Alice Armington: guilty of murder—as charged.

Sentence: live with it.

Both Tex Bodine and Clay Bradford have been in touch by phone several times since I've been back in Houston.

Clay has called at least once a week since I retuned to my condo. In fact he's planning to visit after the first of the year.

Tex has kept me apprised of the events following that horrible afternoon in October and also passed along some of the information revealed in the discovery phase of the Devering case.

Cielo Azul was immediately impounded by the government and will go on the auction block as soon as the Deverings are found guilty—which shouldn't take long. The two were speedily indicted and are now in an El Paso jail awaiting trial set for the first of the year.

Unfortunately, the future of Ola Azul remains up in the air since it falls under the jurisdiction of the Mexican government.

And Ramón Talavera, like most of the other drug trafficking big fish, remains safely across the border in Mexicali with his lovely wife Nita and his five children.

There is one piece of really good news that has come out of this sordid mess. Senior Deputy Ricardo Santana won the Sheriff's election with a write-in vote. It was a landslide.

I check my watch. Almost 1:30. Dinner's at 2:00. So far so good.

And so far it has been a lovely day.

Last night a cold front swept the humidity hovering above the Oz-like skyscrapers of Houston into the middle of the Gulf, leaving a beautiful Colorado-like blue sky, which is predicted to linger through the weekend.

Angela surprised us all by producing, from Illinois, the entire Other Armington clan—fondly referred to as the "OAs,"—to spend the holiday.

We haven't seen that part of our family since Angela's wedding at a lovely Episcopal Church on the North Shore, Christmas a year ago.

Dad's brother, Aiden, and his wife, Sallie, along with Alan and Ardythe and their families are staying with Mother and Dad at the nearby Remington Hotel.

I'm sharing the twin-bedded suite over Angela and Duncan's garage with Arlene, the cousin I'm closest to.

I really enjoy Arlene. She and I have about the same IQ and the same skewed outlook on life. She's also very funny, though she has always insisted that I'm funnier than she is.

I'm so grateful she could come. I desperately needed the comic relief and the gossip she provides from her catbird seat as an independent broker at the Chicago Board of Trade.

We've spent a lot of time reminiscing about the summers we spent together on Fourth Lake in the Adirondacks.

Those talks have been a godsend. For the first time since the incident in New Mexico, I've been able to concentrate on something other than that tragedy.

And I've been able to start looking again toward a future. I've accepted an invitation from the OAs to visit them at their Adirondack compound in June, even though I'm also carrying some baggage associated with that place. Maybe I'll be able to put aside more than one old hurt this coming summer.

At two I take my designated seat across the dining table from my mother who is dandling D3 on her knee.

Though mother holds him securely around his waist with both hands, she isn't supporting his baby head, and it bobbles comically in response to her rhythms.

No one has asked me to dandle D3 on my knee, and I'm just as happy not to put my hands around his satiny, squishy, little waist, or count his delicate baby fingers and toes. I'm not ready to surrender to that exquisite but torturous task just yet.

Duncan and Uncle Aiden sit on either side of my dad who is carving the turkey while explaining in excruciating detail the art of the proper dissection of a wild bird.

Dad always "harvests" a wild turkey or two for Thanksgiving saying it's the Texas pioneer spirit in the Armington blood. Never mind the fact that my father grew up on Lake Michigan and decided to stay in Texas only after a brief stint at Fort Hood where he met my mother.

Poor Duncan. Like Prince Charles and the Queen, he will be doomed to watch my dad carve the bird every Thanksgiving until he makes his final departure. As things stand now Dad will be around until D3 is old enough to take over the job.

I think back to Duncan's first Lampasas Thanksgiving with our family. We were newly engaged back then and my father was overjoyed at the prospect of having a "son" at last.

I remember being extremely peeved about that because I had been Dad's "son" ever since the first time he took me hunting.

And then I met Bill Cotton. That was the end of Duncan.

Who would have guessed that Duncan's "end" would last only a little more than a year? Suddenly, he was back in the family again as Angela's fiancé. Then he was her doting husband, and, finally, the father of the first son of the next Bruce generation.

Somehow I make it through our annual family ritual even though the turkey tastes like sawdust, the rutabaga like rancid turnips, and mother's homemade cranberry relish, so yummy that I have often dreamed about it, a slimy, lumpy, tasteless paste.

The only food that finally makes it Thanksgiving for me is the pumpkin pie that mother makes with canned pumpkin. I grew up loving pumpkin pie from the can.

I know I shouldn't drink while taking anti-depressants, but the pinot noir Duncan has been crowing about for the last three days slides down very nicely to give me a slight buzz, and I'm able to make it through the next hour with a pleasant smile pasted on my face. I know, because I can see my reflection in the glass of a portrait on the wall straight across. And because I suddenly can't remember who that is in the portrait.

Did I ever know?

Will I know again?

CHAPTER 58

I'VE JUST RETURNED TO THE TABLE after removing the last of the dessert plates, when the doorbell begins to chime.

Damn! Has Angela taken it upon herself to invite Dr. Solomon for coffee and dessert? I was so hoping for a weekend of respite from his gentle but annoying probes.

My first thought is to scuttle quickly out of the dining room and hide in the kitchen.

Then I realize that the footsteps, though familiar, don't belong to Dr. Solomon after all.

Tex Bodine, in stonewashed jeans and designer boots, with cowboy hat in hand, appears in the door to the dining room bearing a large bouquet of chrysanthemums—a long-lost friend who has popped in for a surprise visit.

Everybody leaves the table to surround our new guest, except my mother who doesn't exactly know what to do with D3, and myself who needs the next few seconds to struggle with my conflicted emotions. Of course I'm glad to see Tex, but seeing him will open wounds far from healed.

After Angela takes the mums, Duncan shoves a bourbon and branch in Tex's empty hand saying he was told in advance what Bodine's preferred poison was, then leads him to the chair next to mine.

My mother lifts D3 toward Duncan. "If you'll take the baby, I'll get up and leave these two to themselves.

I clamp my mouth shut to keep it from falling open. Those are the first pleasant words she's spoken in my presence during the entire weekend. The rest of the time she has either completely ignored me or made cryptic comments about my "condition" to whoever will listen.

Tex waits until my mother disappears, then settles next to me, and leans to plant a gentle kiss on my cheek. "How's it going?"

I shake my head, push the tears away, and croak, "Some days are better than others. But now that you're here, this will be one of the best."

When his arm circles my shoulders and pulls me to him, I nestle my head against his neck. I haven't let anyone this close to me since Bill died. Hold on. I need to amend that to—since I shot and killed Bill.

Not that anyone else in the family has offered to hug me up. The Armingtons are sort of a stiff-upper-lip tribe.

I pull away and crack a small smile. "Thanks for the hug. I haven't had one in a long, long time."

Tex smiles. "Come to think of it, my desert's been a little arid, too. So, tell me. How are you getting along?"

I can see that his glass has only a few sips left, so I give him the condensed version.

"I'm trying to look ahead instead of dwelling on that horrible day. Really, I am. Actually, I'm toying with becoming a Private Investigator, though I'm in love with the title 'Forensic Investigator.'"

His eyebrows shoot up. "You mean you want to do that crime scene routine like CSI? Nothin' but dead people? Yech!"

"No. No dead bodies. That's not what I'm interested in."

"Accounting investigation?"

"What?"

"Forensics can mean accounting investigation, like tracing large sums of money that have been pilfered and then stashed some place?"

"Uh-ohh. Math was never my strong suit. You should see my checkbook. Or maybe not."

"Then I guess Private Investigator is your best bet. Sounds like a good plan to me." Now, his eyes soften. "You know, I went to Rebbie's funeral."

"Yes, you told me."

"I did? Sorry, I remember thinking maybe I shouldn't."

"You told me what a comfort her son was and how he thanked you for being there for her. That was a wonderful thing for a young man just out of high school to do, wasn't it?"

Tex wipes his eyes with the heels of his hands then lets out a shuddering breath. "Sorry about that. Some days are harder than others."

I watch as Tex struggles to regain his composure, and, after a few seconds pass, he drains the last of his drink, sets down the glass, and in a low voice says, "Allie, the real reason for my visit is. . ."

He lets out his breath, then takes a deep inhale before he continues. "I've taken it upon myself to do something that you might not like, but. . ."

The front door slams and above staccato steps crossing the marble entry hall, I hear Angela's hysterical screech. "Does anyone happen to know who's in that car parked at the front door?"

When she makes it to the dining room door, her face is clotted with rage. "It's that ballsy bitch, Nigella Devering, that's who."

Tex quickly rises and holds out his hand to take mine. "I wish I could have had a little more time to explain, but what Angela says is true. Nigella is in the car. And she wants to see you."

He pulls me to stand as I struggle to make sense out of my sister's pronouncement and Tex's words.

Angela holds up her cell phone and waves it in the air. "I'm calling the police."

Tex drags me behind him as he tries to grab for her cell. "Hold it, Angela. Before you go and do something really stupid, there's a very good reason why Nigella is here."

Angela swings her phone away from his reach. "I thought she was locked up in the El Paso jail."

"She was and she will be again, as soon she's done speaking to Allie."

Angela isn't buying. "Why should I believe you? FYI you never passed my smell-test."

Tex drops his hold on my hand to clench then unclench his fists a few times before he mutters, "And FYI I'm with the FBI and we've been working our tails off to be sure these yahoos are locked up for good."

Duncan materializes to defuse the argument by sliding his arm around Angela's waist. "Calm down, darling. Tex called me earlier this week to ask permission for this visit and once he gave me the details, I agreed."

Angela's chin juts. "Without consulting me?"

"I'm sorry I didn't tell you before now, but with Thanksgiving only a few days away, I didn't want you to worry unnecessarily."

I finally find my voice. "Nigella? Here?"

Tex nods. "If you say it's okay, I'll go get her"

CHAPTER 59

TEX IS BRINGING NIGELLA to the west terrace, still touched by the waning afternoon sun. That's where Duncan suggested the three of us meet.

It wasn't easy for Duncan to persuade Angela that she wasn't to be included, but when he reminded her that the rest of the family was gathered in the living room waiting for her to lead the family's traditional Thanksgiving charades, she grumbled a 'goodbye' and vanished.

I settle on one of the four outdoor chairs surrounding a low table, and wait for Tex to lead Nigella through the wrought-iron gate into the west garden.

When they appear, I suppress a shiver. Here is my nemesis—the woman who stole my love from me.

I can't help but gasp. Nigella, a shadow of her former self, wears a rumpled beige jumpsuit, an abrupt departure from her usual chic attire. Her hair hangs limp to her shoulders and there's not a shred of makeup.

I notice she's rubbing her wrists. But, of course she is, as a federal prisoner, she has been cuffed ever since she left her cell in El Paso.

Nigella lowers herself into the chair closest to mine, as Tex stations himself across the table from us to assume a military stance. His arms are crossed, his weapon is in hand, and Nigella's handcuffs hang from his belt.

After the last light of the day fades and the porch lights spring to life, Nigella gives me a wan smile and says in her familiar Bermudan accent, "I must say this isn't exactly the way I had hoped to see your fair city."

When I don't reply, she glances at Tex, then lowers her eyes. "I thought it would be much easier than this."

Tex slides his weapon up his arm and checks his watch. "You have fifteen minutes before we have to leave. Get on with it. Or I will. Your choice, Devering."

Nigella looks at Tex and shakes her head. "No. No. I want to be the one. I owe her that."

She straightens, spends a few seconds smoothing the wrinkled cotton over her thighs, and finally says, "Long ago back in Lampasas you were very kind to me when others weren't. Do you remember?"

How could I forget? Angela hated that poor girl from the moment she set eyes on her. Poor Nigella. A real fish out of water. Thick glasses. Pasty face. Thin straggly hair. I remember how I made an extra effort to be friendly to make up for my sister's vicious vendetta.

"And because you were once so kind, I thought I might in some small way return the favor."

I finally find my voice. "By doing what?"

"Tex paid me a visit last week and told me that you haven't been at all well."

She raises her eyebrows in anticipation of an answer from me but none comes. I'm still too busy trying to figure out why she's here.

Nigella lets out a long breath. "First off, I want to tell you that I didn't know anything about you and Bill. I mean that you were romantically involved. Not until that day."

For the first time since the shooting I intentionally replay that terrible scene: Bill trains his weapon on me, but I'm not alarmed. Then as he gives me that endearing smile, his right hand flexes and a strange look crosses his face. That's when I squeeze the trigger.

Again, she waits for me to say something, but when I shrug, she hurries on. "I mean I was aware that Nigey sent him to Houston, but I didn't know you were living there. Bill told me it was about the shipment." She flashes me a nervous smile. "As you know, he could be very persuasive as well as secretive."

Tex clears his throat. "Tick. Tock."

"Yes, I know. I know."

When Nigella reaches to touch my hand, I jerk it away. "Just tell me what you're here for."

Her eyes glisten but her words are steady. "I have to tell you the truth about that day. Bill was armed. When he raised his weapon, I heard a click, a misfire. Then you shot."

She hurries on. "When I realized Bill was dead, I hated you for killing him. I wanted to hurt you somehow—make you pay.

"I pushed the gun off the steps before I rushed down the stairs at you."

I give her a suspicious look. "You didn't have time."

"But I did. Tex was standing behind me and you were looking down at your gun. It just took a second."

I look at Tex who shakes his head. "When she told me this last week, I flew up there with a forensic team who covered the area with a metal detector. No luck. But anything could have happened.

"Kids playing in the area. Anything."

"I took a lie detector test, Allie. I passed."

I whirl on Nigella. "You could be a pathological liar. They pass tests easy. Why are you lying?"

She jerks back eyes wide. "But I'm not lying. Why would I offer to take the test? Why would I come all this way? I have nothing to gain from telling you this.

"As I said, I want to repay you for what you did for me in Lampasas. Please, Allie. You have to believe me. Please."

Arlene is snoring. Too much wine, I guess.

After Tex left with Nigella, Angela insisted on opening a couple of Veuve Cliquot to celebrate, and that's what we did.

It doesn't matter that Arlene sounds like a buzz saw. I can't sleep anyway. Even though there's still a gnawing sense of "maybe" at one side of my mind. There's still too much to absorb. Too much to think through.

Maybe, I think, maybe.

Maybe in this life sometimes things fall into your lap, and other times they fall right out of it.

¿Quien sabe?

WWW.LOUISEGAYLORD.COM